The HIDDEN

The HIDDEN

CANDIDA BAKER

KNOPF

A Knopf Book
Published by
Random House Australia Pty Ltd
20 Alfred Street, Milsons Point, NSW 2061
http://www.randomhouse.com.au

Sydney   New York   Toronto
London   Auckland   Johannesburg

First published 2000

National Library of Australia
Cataloguing-in-Publication Entry

Baker, Candida, 1955– .
   The hidden.

   ISBN 1 74051 0119.

   I. Title.

A823.3

Cover and internal photography by Candida Baker
Design by Gayna Murphy/Greendot Design
Typeset in 12/14 pt Bembo by Midland Typesetters, Maryborough,
   Victoria
Printed and bound by the Australian Book Connection

10 9 8 7 6 5 4 3 2 1

For my sister Charlie,
and for Doug

PROLOGUE

A photograph is not only an image (as a painting is an image), an interpretation of the real; it is also a trace, something directly stencilled off the real, like a footprint or a death mask.

Susan Sontag

So these are the memories I sort. Gum trees and blue skies, a particular dusty shade of green, difficult to describe, hard to photograph.

'Will you?' asked the gallery. 'Everybody's interested in your early work. We'd love to do an exhibition.'

I agreed. I thought: *Perhaps enough time has passed.* I thought that if I sorted the photographs I could sort the events, I could make sense of *life* as well. I think there was the faintest suggestion that if I could render down Australia, I could make it all un-happen. I would neatly arrange photographs on the plain white gallery walls, and people would see and buy them and hang them on their walls. I would part with the photographs, which are part of the story; and because they, the audience, would have no idea about the story, by their act of purchasing they would render it into nothing and thereby release me.

Harry is curious about what I'm doing. 'You've never talked about Australia much, Mum,' he says.

No, well.

Harry is twenty now, which means that it is approximately twenty years and nine months ago that these events happened.

He has a girlfriend. They sleep together here often. They raid the fridge and play CDs too loudly, and he leaves his gigantic shoes exactly where I will trip over them when I stumble out of my darkroom, but I am happy to have him here. I don't tell him I can hear him and Karen making love through the bedroom wall. It is a strange thing lying there partnerless, a fifty-five-year-old woman, listening to your son making love.

I invented a father for him. I told him that I met his father in Greece when I was there taking photographs for a magazine, and that it was a holiday fling. I told him, when he was still small enough to bombard me with questions, that I didn't even know his father's last name, that I had tried to send letters to him, and they had always been returned, unopened. In the end, he stopped asking. There was one photograph of a man, in shadow on the corner of a street in Athens. I told him that was his father, and he has it framed in his room.

Has he ever wondered why he doesn't look the least bit Greek? Why he is so tall and blond and Anglo? He has never mentioned it.

Still, Harry is incidental; accidental and incidental to the story. It was not his story even if it created him. I have come to believe during my life that all of us have one story to tell – many have more, of course – but we all have one. It is a shadow we are born with and it shapes our destinies. This was my shadow.

I have never wanted to write it down before, but looking day after day at these photographs I have felt my mortality whispering in the corner and thought that one day Harry should know, so that he can make his choices, as I came to make mine. And so I, who have avoided pen and paper all my life, have decided that this is what I will do. I will write it, and perhaps by doing so I will finally be rid of it forever.

Chapter ONE

The optical arts spring from the eye and solely
from the eye.

Jules Laforgue, 'Impressionism'

Why do we look at an image? More specifically, why do we look at a photographic image? For two reasons, I believe. The first is that even if we are witnessing distortion, a photograph reminds us of what we perceive to be reality. The second, which is an interesting dichotomy, is that a photograph, I would suggest, triggers a symbolic reaction; despite its much vaunted connection to supposed reality it reaches beyond logic. I suppose one could even ask: What is the purpose of a photograph? It is many years since I have asked myself that question. Perhaps once my answer would have been to do with 'art' or 'technique' or a way of seeing. Now I think it would be both more simple and more complex. I think the purpose of a photograph is to bring the dark into the light, to make the hidden seen.

I hold a photograph in my hand, and it is of daffodils. Why I liked to look at this image – why I still like to look at it – is that when I took it, it had just stopped raining. There is moisture on the petals and there is a sense to an European eye at least, used to daffodils in greener pastures, of something slightly odd – the grey green gum trees behind the flowers give the hint of a landscape folding into ... what? Not an English country garden, at any rate.

This is what *I* remember:

The lichen sparkled. There was sun after the rain. A rock wallaby paused; I thought it was a kangaroo. 'No,' he told me, 'it's a wallaby. Darker and smaller.' Its ears went back, forward. We were up on a hill above a farmhouse, the man and the woman. We drove carefully down the track, and there were the daffodils, all around the shabby house. They had tiny pendants of moisture on the ribbon furling of their petals. The woman got her camera out.

If I was to try and imagine what *he* might remember, it might be this:

'Oh my darling, it's lovely.'

She called to him as she leant over the daffodils. The way her hair fell. Like the other one, but she was not the other one. The farmhouse, so still and silent, seemed to be reproaching him for his absence. 'So there you are,' it said, as he began the unpacking, while his new wife got her camera out.

Is this fair to both of us? At least I think it is not unfair.

The windows were stuck. We had to push and prise them, before the handles suddenly gave way and the windows shot up. We both laughed, gulping in the sudden gust of fresh air in the dusty rooms.

'I swear you can taste the wattle, Paul,' the woman said. Behind her he grumbled as he unloaded boxes. 'You'd think we'd come for a year.' But she could tell he was pleased that she'd been thoughtful. The extra things she'd bought on top of his groceries: Amaretto biscuits, a bottle of brandy. She took over the unpacking, exploring the cupboards.

I enjoyed it, I'll admit. After all, we were there on our honeymoon. We'd talked about where we might go. Somewhere exotic and tropical . . . Bali perhaps. Somewhere autumnal and European . . . the south of France perhaps. But in the end he'd asked, 'What do you think – I'd love to go to the farm. Could you handle it?' And I'd agreed. I was in love with him, in love with the landscape. I couldn't imagine leaving Australia at this time. It was all exciting and new and we were in love, so why not?

So there we were and he sat on the verandah and smoked a cigarette, and I put things away, cereal here, coffee there. I felt a small tingle of possession. I knew, of course, that it had been their home too, but after all it was not as if I had broken up the marriage. (Or that is what I thought at the time.)

I remember wondering what he was thinking about while he sat on the verandah gazing into the middle distance. Would I be right in saying that he was thinking about her? I think I will make it so anyway.

Let's say he was waiting. Perhaps even thinking about waiting.

He thought, as he sat on the verandah, about women. How men waited for them, were always waiting for them to finish something, anything. Women to finish talking, women to dress, women to arrive, women to leave, women to come back. But this time there was no coming back. It would never be as it was before. Before he did not smoke, now he did. If she were going to be anywhere it would be here, wouldn't it? He leant forward to listen for the sound of her voice on the wind.

That is how the woman saw him. Leaning forward, his body tensed. Suddenly cold fingers of doubt grabbed the nape of her neck. The thought crossed her mind: This was another woman's place.

He turned and smiled at me. 'Lunch?' I said.

The word photograph means literally light-writing. It speaks of the central concern of photography which is, of course, the control of light and time. Joseph Nicephore Niepce's heliograph, *View from a Window at Gras*, taken in 1826, had an eight-hour exposure. The result was an impressionistic blur, disappointing enough for Niepce to team up with another Frenchman, Louis-Jacques-Mande Daguerre. The daguerrotype caused Delacroix to lament, 'From this day, painting is dead'. There was another development too, of course, Fox Talbot's 'photogenic drawings' created by placing objects between a photosensitive surface and a light source. The heliograph provided the photographic world with realism, the photogenic drawings with somewhat more original but, perhaps one could argue, also less successful practices such as the photogram.

Caroline Savage could tell you her life story in eight hours. Give or take. Or I could if I wanted. Imagine that: an entire day passing while one photograph was taken. In that first afternoon I was so excited I shot rolls of film. I had not been in Australia long. I had never seen an

Australian farm. I was fascinated by the bleached bones lying everywhere, by the ringbarked trees and outcrops of shale. It was not that bright blue sky I associate with my time there, that first day. The light was grey and soft, almost English, which to my unaccustomed eyes made the landscape even more incongruous.

After lunch we walked.

'Here,' he said, 'you may as well take Ellen's anorak. In case it rains.'

I did not like to say, But I do not want to wear a dead woman's clothes.

The bush smelled of mint and animal droppings and we went quietly, looking for goats.

'We'll smell them first,' the man said, as they headed over the hill. But it was almost simultaneous, the sighting and the smelling, leaving both sides startled, the couple laughing, the goats bounding away, kids scrabbling to keep up on the sheer cliffs.

'They're so sweet.'

'Aren't they though? The kids taste good too. I'll get us one soon.'

'Don't do that.' The woman stroked his arm. 'They're too beautiful.'

'Bloody nuisance,' he said. 'They're a bloody nuisance.' But she could tell he was touched by her admiration of them.

The rain came again. Sudden and fierce. Stinging our cheeks so that I was pleased to have the coat. We sheltered under a tree. 'It suits you, that colour,' Paul said.

I would not want anybody to think that I was a soft photographer. I'd done my share of wars – the Middle East, the obligatory corpses, landmine victims, et cetera. As a young photographer I had always fancied myself as the next Margaret Bourke-White. I mean she was *the* role model for female photographers. How sad that *Life* and *Fortune* no longer exist. But despite a flourishing news career, landscape photography has always been a private passion. Also, if I am to be honest, in the end I think I do not have the stomach for too much brutality. I have never, like some photographers I've known, got used to war, or death or corpses, or mutilation. (Actually, I would contend that no-one ever gets used to it, some people are simply more able to be somewhat brutalised by it, to practise a detachment which gradually becomes their reality. Even Capa – despite the fact that his work is an attack on the supposed glamour of war – in the end he could not live without it himself. In 1954 he went to Vietnam. He was on patrol with the French when he stepped on a landmine and died with his final pictures in his camera. He had carved the iconography of the last Great War and died in a prescient moment, in the land-scape of an as yet untold war.) I was never quite as keen, if the truth be known, as some of my colleagues, on pushing myself to the utmost limits of survival simply to send an image back to an armchair-based editor who might or might not reject it. I suppose that is why I have become more settled since I took up a permanent position at the college. Perhaps if I'd had the talent I might have become a landscape artist, but over the years I have come to believe that landscape photography can carry just as much freight as a good painting. Still, none of my photographs from that afternoon will make the final cut. They are all too gentle. Pretty, almost. But that is how I was feeling that day, soft and sentimental. To this day, I have no idea why the weekend supplement magazine I occasionally filed for asked me to do a photo-essay on Australia. But they did, and I accepted. I met Paul in Sydney and much to both our surprises we fell in love. I flew back, filed my photo-essay, sorted out my life — that did not take much doing, I'd been living out of a suitcase for years — flew back to Sydney and got married. And we lived happily ever after. Except we didn't.

So you see I have given you much more information in one page than I could in one photograph. You know stuff about me now. But for me the problem is that words do not adequately resonate. For me every photograph is a story. And yet there are areas, aren't there? How do you photograph sex, the awkward act of it, without somehow demeaning it? That is hard. The body itself poses difficulties most photographers never come to terms with, particularly of course the female body. (I am not talking pornography here, that is another matter.) My belief is that Alfred Stieglitz has come closer than anyone to defining the inherent sensuality in the female form with a respect for what you do not see — the brain, the wit, the intelligence, the personality. He photographed Georgia O'Keefe, his second wife, for twenty-seven years. I remember when I first heard that, I was astonished that anybody would want to photograph the same person year in, year out. That was before I fell in love, and before I was a mother.

What I am avoiding here is the subject of sex. I have to tell you, it was good, very good. In fact so good that if things had worked out differently perhaps I would have photographed Paul for twenty-seven years. Try as I might and despite everything, I am unable to eradicate the memory of that first night in the farmhouse. Let's face it, I don't want to eradicate it. The memory of good sex is not to be sneered at, after all.

I remember that he was impressed that I could use a wood stove. I cooked chicken casserole and apple pie. (Did I? I don't know. But it sounds realistic, and I used to cook both those things.) I grew up with a wood stove, I told him, in the country, in England. In fact, if someone was to ask me what my strongest childhood memories were, it would be easy: gumboots, getting water from the well, the hip bath, the old copper boiler and the wood stove. That just about sums it all up. Oh, and my pony, of course.

After dinner we sat in front of the fire. He was in the chair, I was at his feet. He stroked my hair, and when he bent to kiss me I almost exploded.

In bed the rain drummed on the tin roof. It was as if he was mapping me, learning the contours of my body. His detachment was erotic, I have to say. He kissed me, my armpits, eyelids, my belly button. When he went down on me I came almost instantly. Then it was my turn to explore him, to take him in my mouth. Was I someone else for him? Even now that idea hurts. But I don't think so. I don't think she had recaptured him then. I think he belonged to me heart and soul that night, and me to him.

She woke early while he was still sleeping. His hand was thrown across his eyes. Caroline watched him. Did he dream of her still? He spoke of her from time to time. She encouraged it, of course. After all it was only fourteen months ago. Nobody close to her had ever died. She had become middle-aged without anybody close to her dying. (*Although it is my belief that divorce is a kind of death for children. At least it had been for me.*) How must it be? He only told her things. Ellen liked this, did this. No feelings, no photos, almost no evidence of a life.

Personally I do not like photography that is devoid of feeling. What I mean by that is a certain coldness or over-explanation. I would take, for instance, an Ansel Adams object over a Robert Mapplethorpe portrait any day. It is why I always encourage my students to photograph those subjects that engage their feelings, even that most clichéd of areas, their families. Whatever, as they say, turns you on.

I now can't tell if it is retrospective or current knowledge that there was an absence of photographs of Ellen. At the time Paul and I seemed equally caught up in the business of being in love. I can't remember, and yet it would have been odd for me even all those years ago not to notice that absence. Did I, for instance, notice that when we got married we only invited a handful of people? At the time it seemed natural to want something small and intimate. But now I wonder if perhaps he was even then keeping me at arm's length, just a little. I think he did not want all his old friends replacing Ellen in their minds with me.

The woman slipped out of bed and pulled on her clothes, carefully shutting the bedroom door behind her. In the early morning light, the house seemed forlorn, all the cheer of the fire and the evening gone. When Caroline ran her finger along the mantelpiece it left a clean trail through the dust. In the bathroom everything was cold – the toilet, the sink, even the handle of her toothbrush. She rubbed her hands on her arms to warm herself and set off into the morning.

Just as she was about to close the door, she picked up the anorak.

She followed a track.

'You can go as far as the eye can see,' he had said. 'It's all ours.'

Not the best country, he'd explained. Not rubbish country, but not the best. Perfect for running merinos, some fine wool to be had off them. Every now and then he even made a bit of money out of it. But that was not the point. The point was, it was a getaway. Caroline breathed deeply, swinging her arms. The track led to a hill overlooking a valley. Yesterday they had seen the river running far below. From their vantage point it had been hard for her to accept that the small grey marbles she could see were in fact huge boulders flanking the sides of the river.

'You should see them when you get down,' he'd said. 'We'll take a picnic lunch, go in the Toyota.'

But this morning the valley was covered in fog. The river had disappeared into a grey sea running between the hills. Caroline was tempted to step out into it, to be absorbed by that soft greyness. It seemed as if it must hold her. The tortured branches of tree skeletons rose up like praying hands reaching towards air. A wedge-tailed eagle soared above her. She marvelled in it and touched the earth – her earth – with her hands.

★

In some ways, when I write like this, of Caroline, I feel somewhat as if I am betraying her by saying *she* and *her*. And yet there is this: I am not the Caroline she was. Perhaps if the story I am telling here was less disturbing I would not feel this distance between us, perhaps it would be simple to use *I*. Is the third person, too, a way of distancing myself from my reactions? I didn't think at the time that thirty-five was young. Now, at fifty-five, I look back in disbelief at Caroline's naiveté.

My father rang me the other day to tell me that he had been diagnosed with lung cancer. He said: 'Early days, Caro, don't worry. They tell me it's very early.' He was more distressed that he had to go into some kind of scanning machine. 'I told them I get claustrophobia. They tried to point out that it couldn't be worse than the cancer, but I don't know.'

He gets claustrophobia because his older brother locked him in an ottoman when my father was four and his brother was six. His brother wandered off and forgot about him.

'I don't blame him,' he said.

'No,' I said, 'but it's cause and effect, isn't it?'

There was a slight pause and he said, Yes that was it, no blame but cause and effect. Suddenly I felt like saying that this is how I feel about him, no blame but cause and effect, but there has been too much misunderstanding for me even to try.

If I were to attempt it I might say you left, and you were absent and the effect on me was that I was not good at choosing men who might stay. (Oh, and let me double that. I have not been good at staying, however much it might hurt to admit it.) Perhaps if he had not left Paul may never even have occurred. But then of course, I would have to accept that Harry too would not be here, and that is unthinkable.

While I was out walking on that track, inhaling the early morning smells, feeling the earth in my hands, what was Paul doing? Did he shift in the bed, throw out an arm to where my body should have been? Was it my name or hers he whispered? I think it was hers. I think in his sleep she came and stole him away from me.

'Ellen,' he whispered. 'Ellen.'

He sat up and covered his face with his hands, crying like a baby, swaying backwards and forwards, his arms held tight around himself.

And yet. He was not all gone, not straight away. I wandered back to the house, picking wildflowers and sprays of gum. As I got to the top of the hill I could smell the fresh coffee. 'That was wishful thinking,' he teased me. But it was true, and there was bacon and eggs for breakfast, and a daffodil in a vase in the middle of the table.

After breakfast we sat on the verandah. He was leafing through a folder. I said I'd like to visit Rock Forest.

'Why?'

I shrugged. 'To look around, buy some postcards, maybe take the camera.'

'Okay,' he said. 'If you like.'

Was there just the slightest moment of hesitation in his voice?

I'll tell you a couple of tricky things about photography. One is trying to raise yourself above a perceived expectation of what a place, or a person, or an object will choose to reveal of itself to you. The other is – and perhaps this is part of the same problem – trying to capture the essence of what you are photographing. If indeed this is actually wholly possible, which I doubt.

Take, for instance, New York. I think no-one would argue with the notion that New York is a photographic icon. At some point, if you are a photographer, you will want to go there, to try your luck, to see if you can find something of the Berenice Abbott within yourself, or perhaps Walker Evans. Even if you are not a photographer, if you visit New York, you will take pictures there. In the 1930s Berenice Abbott decided almost literally to photograph the whole of New York. Just anything and everything. But in the end New York still refuses to reveal itself completely to Abbott's probing. You could take them all, Thompson, Abbott, Evans, Arbus, Sherman, Meyerovitz, Leibovitz . . . on and on and on. And yet if you were a New Yorker who had lived there all your life, you might still say, Well, that is interesting, but it is not *my* New York, it is not what *I* see.

I had – it seems funny now – an expectation around the word 'historic'. The Australian notion of historic – a word liberally applied to anything more than fifty years old – can be quite unsettling to a newcomer.

The idea of photographing a gold town was appealing to Caroline. She imagined it somehow still complete, just minus the people, but when they reached Rock Forest, she was put out. The houses upset her. They leant dangerously. They seemed neglected, somehow desolate. A few were simply shanties made of corrugated iron. In the shop, with its dusty collection of souvenir spoons and groceries that had seen better days, Paul introduced her to the shopkeeper. The man, he looked part-Asian, stared straight through her and mumbled something.

Driving back out to the farm, Caroline couldn't bring herself to speak.

'What's wrong?' But he knew. Of course he knew. He'd felt the stares from behind the curtains, heard the silence fall as they walked past the hotel. He'd called out g'day, as he always had, but even old Tom in his rocking chair had been silent.

She blurted out, she didn't mean to, but couldn't help herself: 'Why were they so unfriendly?'

'I don't know, love.' He frowned. 'They were all fond of Ellen.'

So just then at that precise moment when we were trying to recover ourselves from this ripple – the tiny misunderstandings, the vague air of hostility – there was this tremendous racket, noise and dust and a screech of brakes. An old truck hurtled past us, dangerously close. As it went by I could just glimpse the driver, a thickset man with a beard. He raised his hand and smiled.

'Well,' I said, 'at least he's friendly.'

And Paul was silent.

And even all this time later, I have no idea what he was thinking at that precise moment. I could not, even in this self-confessional mode, hazard a guess.

I know this though, that as we got nearer the property, I felt genuinely happy again. As if I was returning home. And somehow my reference map was readjusting itself. I was seeing images of Rock Forest in my mind, but this time really seeing them, so they were not what I was expecting, so what? Those shanties, the cows in the street, the whole air of neglect – it was a ghost town, not a gold town, but its gold might reveal itself to me in a different light.

I climbed out of the car to open the gate.

'You go ahead,' I said. 'I'll walk back.'

Poised with the camera. A shot rang out. Startled roos took off from their resting places, heading towards the horizon. Looking up towards the truck Caroline saw the driver's door was open and Paul was standing by his gun.

'It's okay,' he called. 'Just a rabbit.'

Caroline waved, pantomimed her beating heart, turned back to her work.

Chapter TWO

'The camera cannot lie . . .' Discuss this statement. Do you think it is true or false? Support
your argument with examples. Is it possible for
this to be both true and false? Discuss the changing nature of technology and its effect upon
photography.

CS: essay questions for second-year students

I say I don't put pen to paper, but of course as a teacher
I must do that. I suppose what I would say is I am not
one for writing down feelings, or wanting to attempt anything other than the writing needed to create efficiency. I
have always labelled, which is quite different. I file all my
essay questions, I caption all my photographs – everything
is in chronological order – and beside my filing cabinets
filed first by category and then alphabetically is every
country, person, place or thing I have ever photographed.

I have always felt a need to label. An astrologer who

16

once did my chart told me it was the influence of having Virgo as a rising sign. I resisted the explanation somewhat but she was adamant. She said, 'You can't be happy until you feel you have grappled with life and filed it away, and that is preventing you from happiness because, of course, it is impossible to file life.' I was young enough to believe there was nothing in what she said, and I still have trouble accepting that something as random as the position of a star can account for a filing habit. I put it down to when my father left home, and he would send me postcards that I would stick into a scrapbook with the date underneath. Labels equalled control, I suppose. An attempt to prove He Was There. I Was Here. He Sent Me Postcards.

But the other sort of writing – love letters, dreams, poems, even personal notes – I have never gone in for. They can bounce back and hit you in all sorts of ways.

We had been at the farm for two days when I found a note. Is it necessary to say that Paul and I were happy then? I think so. Even though the story was already waiting in the wings, its talons extended, I think Harry should know, and I should try and remember that we were happy. It never seemed to me to be an odd thing to do, to fall in love and marry in a matter of months. As a photographer each job you do obsesses you while you do it, and when we moved so quickly from meeting to marriage I simply threw myself into the relationship, and so did Paul. He seemed so definite and sure of himself in comparison to English men. He was funny and warm and kind to me. If I ever thought about Ellen and their relationship it was to be grateful that he had learnt to cohabit with someone, that he knew more about it than me. After all, I knew I had managed to avoid commitment thus far, and yet part of me had longed for it – for marriage, for a family, for the whole kit and caboodle. Perhaps by falling in love in Australia it made the whole relationship process less threatening. I was not well enough versed in the art of being a couple to read the subtleties that I sense now must have been there. But we were happy, and he was good to me.

There I was then, and I was cleaning out a cupboard, carefully removing everything, wiping down, washing up, putting it all back. There was a small piece of paper on top of a pile of saucers.

Caroline picked up the note. 'Darling,' it read. 'Food in oven. Husband in Bed.' Her heart lurched. She put a hand to her chest as if she had been struck. 'Darling ... Husband ... Bed.' Surely these words were meant for her? She looked around, half expecting to see the person for whom the words were intended.

'Hello,' Ellen might say. 'Thank you for looking after him. So kind of you. You can go now.' Dismissed.

And as I stood there, the note still in my hand, I remember there was a knock on the door, and that for a mad moment, I thought it might be Ellen. But as soon as I opened it I recognised the man from the old truck. And even then I think I felt an odd quiver that he should twice now materialise during a moment of disquiet. At least, if I did not feel it then I certainly felt it soon after.

If I had taken a photograph, this is what you would see. I would have, if it were possible, taken it from behind me. So you would see the dark interior of the kitchen, wood and flagstones and a woman's shape — average height and weight, dark shoulder-length hair — with her back to the camera; an open door in front of her with a glimpse of gum trees and hills, and a man — tall, bearded — filling the door frame, with a dead kangaroo on his shoulder.

'Been meaning to come over,' this man said. 'Brought you both a bit of roo.'

I was shocked. 'Kangaroo?'

'No cholesterol, tasty as anything. They sell it in Harrods these days they tell me. Aren't you going to ask me in?'

And I realised I was flustered. Overcome by the maleness of him, even the smell of him, his workboots, his shirt, the dried blood. Who wouldn't be?

'Of course,' I said. 'Come in. Would you like a cup of tea? Paul's getting some wood.'

'I'd rather have a beer.' He slapped the roo haunch, blood oozing from its leg, down on the marble slab near the stove. Before I could reach the fridge, he was already there. Before I could protest, he was somehow at home, legs up, the beer open.

He looked me up and down. By this time I had recovered myself, and I stared quite calmly back at him, but in truth I did not like the way he looked at me. I have rarely felt more naked.

'Well,' said the man to the woman in front of him. 'You've made it nice here. Anyway, the name's Jim. Jim Stannard. Nice to meet you.'

Caroline held out her hand. 'I'm Caroline, Caroline Savage. I mean, Caroline Lucas.'

He laughed. 'Savage is better, much better. So, what do

19

you expect to do around here? Bit dead for a city person, isn't it? Isn't it?'

'Oh no. I love it . . . the colours, you know. I grew up in the country. I'd like to get a horse, explore the bush.'

He raised an eyebrow. 'Explore the bush. There's a notion. You must be English.'

Caroline felt she should apologise. 'Well, yes, I'm afraid I am.'

'Don't be afraid, love. Funny thing though, both of you English.'

At first I didn't get it. 'No,' I said. 'Paul's not English. He's Australian.'

'Not Paul, Ellen. Ellen was English.'

And then there was a shadow.

'Jim.'

'Paul. How are you mate? Brought you a bit of roo.'

'So I see.'

And then there was a pause.

'Well,' said Jim, putting down his beer. 'I just came round to make your wife's acquaintance. I'll be off then. Wait until shearing's over and we'll get together for a spot of tea.' He stood, holding out his hand, towering over Paul, who had moved beside me. 'You've done well there, Paul. Very well.'

My husband stared into the distance. He did not hold out his hand. 'Thank you.'

'Well,' Jim looked uncomfortable. His hand dropped. 'See you around.'

(A thought occurs to me, that when Harry finally reads this he might well ask me, 'But how do you remember everything they said? How can you be so sure?' And of course, there are some bits where I do not remember exactly what was said, but most of it – well, it's like a film, I've replayed and replayed it for twenty years. I can quote you whole chunks of my life, in much the same way that I once learnt the first ten minutes of Pinter's *Betrayal*, and I can still recite it. I even make my photography students study it. Why? Because I tell them, the opening scene is a masterpiece. It is mundane to the point of banality. Neither of the characters even finishes a sentence, or hardly, and at the same time, it is what they *don't* say that gives you all the information you require.)

One of the reasons I replay my own script is to look for clues. Now I see them everywhere – the semiotics are clear. Then, I did not. Was I stupid? No. I was in love and for the first time in my life I desperately, achingly wanted it to work. I wanted it to be the true love that would sustain me in my life. I wanted it to be The Truth.

Chapter THREE

It is not always the sharpest pictures that give you the most information. If you limit your sharp focus zone, the most important picture element will stand in relief to the rest of the photograph. Think to yourself: What is the message I am trying to convey? What do I want people to see clearly, what do I want to remain hidden?'

CS: notes to first-year students on a field trip to the Lake District

I often wonder about the nature of obsession. It is hard to explain to someone who is not driven, why there is something that comes first, ahead of everything else in your life. How many relationships have I lost because I am a photographer first, a mother second and a partner third? There are people who are driven, and there are people who are not. Those who are not appear to know how to lead normal lives: how to relax, go on holiday, watch television at night, switch their brains off. Those who have fallen prey to obsession have no idea how to do those things. Anything that falls into the so-called normal areas of life is achieved – and that's not too strong a word for it – almost under sufferance. Perhaps some of the answers to my questions lie in this, in an obsessive nature.

Since I was a teenager I have seen a frame around everything. I do it automatically. I do it everywhere, with everyone. I can't help it. I don't think Paul had the slightest idea what that meant when he married me. Eisenstaedt said: 'The world we live in is a succession of fleeting moments, any one of which might say something significant. When such an instant arrives, I react intuitively. There is, I think, an electronic impulse between my eye and my finger. But even this is not enough. I dream that someday the step between my mind and my finger will no longer be needed. And that simply by blinking my eyes, I shall make pictures. Then, I think, I shall *really* have become a photographer.' The first time I read that I was stunned. That's it! I thought, that's me. I was young enough at the time to imagine nothing less than genius in my future. Ah well, time gradually softens that blow.

But then, having sorted out the word historic, I wanted to go back to Rock Forest and Paul was not unsympathetic. 'We'll go to the racecourse,' he said. 'That's where I'd take photos if I was you.' It was a good thing that I had already adjusted my frames of reference. I did not expect to see anything remotely like a racecourse, and it was certainly not any racecourse I had seen before – or since, come to that.

To get there we turned off the Rock Forest road onto a dirt track, past an avenue of spindly gums with trunks as skinny and pale as an old man's legs. Stopping at a ditch, we blinked our way out into the bright sun. Forlorn sheets of tin flapped in the breeze, one nail between them and the dirt. The weathered timber fence which must have once marked the boundaries of the racecourse was now a grey blur between lines of weeds.

I squared my hands and peered through them. I was delighted. 'I'll get my camera,' I said.

And unaccountably Paul was annoyed. I could feel it. 'Do you have to?' he said. 'Can't you just *look* at something?'

'But Paul, it's what I do.' I was surprised. I thought, *He knows that's what I do, that's how we met.* 'I could sell pictures like this anywhere.'

And the annoyance passed as quickly as that. 'Come here,' he said, drawing me to him. He slid his hands over my hips, and kissed me. 'Listen ...'

Caroline strained to hear. 'What? I can't hear anything.'

He moved away from her. 'Yes, you can ... listen ...here they come, around the first bend.' He picked up a twig flicking it against his thigh. 'It's Simply Paul and Princess Caroline in the lead.' He danced and pranced down the dirt track, so that she laughed to see him − almost a child's version of how a horse moves, neck arched, feet up. 'Ghost Town and Tumbleweed are just a length behind. Fallen Fence is nowhere to be seen ... oh, this is a great race! The mare's got it in the bag, and in such heavy going. It's Princess Caroline! Princess Caroline by a neck. Simply Paul just couldn't match the pace.' She blew him kisses, high-stepped it like a winner towards him, and he grabbed her hand. 'Come on.'

They walked towards the disused chutes. In one of the corrals a lizard lay basking in the sun, twitching away at the last minute as they climbed up onto what was once a viewing platform. 'It must have been great once,' Paul said, looking out over the desolate landscape, where the sadness of once-lived lives seemed to hang in the air, in every tree branch. 'Imagine them all here, sweltering away in their Sunday best.'

In the end I could stand it no longer.

'You never told me,' I said.

'I never told you what?'

'That she, that Ellen, was English.'

He stared at the horizon. 'Didn't I? Well, it's not very important after all, is it?'

What could I say? *Yes. No. Of course, of course not.*

The journey back from the racetrack was dusty and hot.

'God.' I wiped my face and neck for the umpteenth time. 'What's it like in summer?'

Paul grinned. 'You sound like Ellen.'

And I remember that I thought, *Thank God he's said her name.* And I was about to say something when Paul slammed on the brakes.

'Shit,' he said.

'What?'

Caroline's eyes followed his pointing hand, towards the sign at the entrance of the property. It was riddled with bullet holes.

'Who would do a thing like that?'

'Local vandals probably,' he said as the truck came to a stop, and he climbed out. 'It's not unknown.'

Apart from his expletives, he seemed, Caroline thought, unconcerned, as if it was not important.

She climbed out too. 'Well, who do we report it to?'

He was busy taking the sign down. 'What?'

'I said, "Who do we report it to?" There must be somebody. Someone local. A policeman.'

Paul straightened up and looked at her. He seemed momentarily amused, almost lovingly so. 'Oh yes,' he said. 'There's somebody, but I don't think he would be too bothered by this. This is the bush, love, not the home counties.'

I am not the first person to point out the relationship between guns and cameras, between the terminology used for each. You shoot someone with a gun, you shoot someone with a camera. If your aim is accurate you could go as far to say that you kill with both. Which is of course why some primitive tribes do not like to have their photographs taken.

I remember once reading about a particularly distressing murder where a gunman shot dead a shopkeeper in front of the man's two children. And I knew, in my mind's eye, that this father had been shot three times. Once by the gunman, and the second time by the police photographer, and the third by the newspapers in which I could now see him. He was triply dead, even the angles of his death immortalised. And I wondered if, over time, what the two children would come to remember about their father would be the photographs of his death rather than him.

But that is as nothing in comparison to Robert Haeberle's *People About to be Shot*, his ferocious image of the 1969 My Lai massacre in Vietnam. I think it is almost more disturbing than Hung Cong (Nick) Ut's *Accidental Napalm Attack*, even though this was perhaps the picture, with the naked girl screaming in terror, that became the seminal image of that war. But it is *People About to be Shot* that I require my students to study. Why? Because it is the sheer ordinary snapshot quality of the picture that gives it its power. A group of people huddled together, obviously in distress, but about to be shot? How can this be? I find that many students simply can't look at it. It is so far out of their terms of reference that they are unable to meet it emotionally. They are unable to understand how a photographer could calmly photograph a group of people, women and girls and children, who the next second will be shot (again) and this time they will be dead. And what are they doing? Some crying, some clinging, some . . . for god's sake one of them adjusting the buttons on her cardigan. I would almost go as far to say that it is with this image that I begin to get an idea of who might or might not make a photographer. Those who can't look at all, who are too distressed or distraught to engage with the image, generally won't, and those who try too hard to be detached, to pretend that this photograph simply doesn't affect them, generally won't. Then there is the last third, the smallest group usually, who will engage with it, despite their distress. Who will talk about it, what the photographer might have been feeling, what the victims/subjects were feeling, what it conjures up for them. And these are the ones I begin to look at with renewed interest, the ones where I think, 'Yes, you might get it. You just might get it.' And then, of course, it is the time to introduce them to Robert

Capa, and in particular to the Republican militiaman, and the debate surrounding that photograph. Let me state here that I simply don't believe he manufactured that photograph, but there will always be those who can't accept that anyone can have so calmly documented the exact moment of someone's death. (Answer me this: if Capa had known he was about to step on a landmine, would he have organised to shoot the moment of his death, somehow? Of course he would have.)

But of course guns are still one thing when they are in images – they are another in reality. I remember that I was upset by the business of the sign. I felt as if somehow we had been – both of us – violated. At that time people in England did not take guns to signposts. I remember that I badgered Paul over dinner about it. I wanted him to report it, to somehow make it safe again.

'Don't you see?' I remember saying. 'There could be someone with a gun out there, waiting for us. I just think we should tell the local policeman.'

And Paul was so quiet, I began to wonder if he was ever going to answer me, until finally he spoke. 'Look,' he said, 'there is no policeman out here. It's too small to warrant one. We'd have to go to Bathurst to report it, and they'd think we were mad. The closest thing to a policeman here is Jim. He works for the parks department, and he's made himself the self-appointed lawman in these parts. The police in Bathurst are happy to let him do it – he keeps the locals under control for them – but he's the only person here we could report this to, and for various personal reasons I don't wish to do that.'

★

Caroline was perturbed. 'But he said he was a shearer. He doesn't, well, he doesn't look like a, whatever it was you said, a parks person.'

'He didn't say he was a shearer. He said he'd call after the shearing, after he's finished his busy season locking all the boys up when they get pissed and shoot the place up. Jim would say it was high spirits,' said her husband, from the other side of the table, from the other side of the planet. 'That's what Jim would say, and he'd be right.'

'But we could still tell him though,' Caroline insisted. 'I still think he should know. He's your friend, isn't he? He'd probably want to know.'

'He's not my friend.' That's what I remember he said, and I said something, 'Well, acquaintance then.' And he said, 'No,' and then he said it again, 'No, no'. It seemed such an odd thing to say, so obviously. . . I don't know – untrue or not right – that I was puzzled, so I waited for what he would say next. When he spoke his face was contorted with pain.

'He found her,' he said. 'He found Ellen. It should have been me, and he got there first.'

Did I have any idea of the levels of guilt and distress I was dealing with? Absolutely not, is the answer. I was sympathetic, I felt for him, I understood why he was reluctant to speak to Jim, but it was about then that I began to realise Ellen was not, in effect, quite as dead as she might be.

So we let it go. Sort of. But as I sat on the verandah, I began to reflect on the last few days. I felt as if I had a huge jigsaw puzzle laid out on a tray in front of me, and I had chanced across a corner, and a few mismatched pieces of sky and ground. Why was it important to me that Paul had not told me Ellen was English? What did it matter? There were plenty of Australians who were originally English, after all. But it was not just that. There was something more subtle. I had noticed this: whenever I moved something in the house, Paul would move it back. It hadn't happened often, it might even have been coincidence, but it was gradually dawning on me that Paul still saw it as Ellen's house.

Yet this was odd in itself, because there was very little there that seemed to belong to her. The only remnants left of Ellen's life at the farmhouse were the anorak, the gumboots and the scarf − all left by the front door as if she might be needing them at any moment. Why had he not thrown those away too? Perhaps because they were her most everyday objects. Perhaps he simply couldn't bear to part with them.

In Sydney there had been nothing, not even an anorak, to suggest a previous relationship. On our second date, before I knew about Ellen, we'd gone back to his place for a drink, and I had been struck by how unlike a bachelor home his place was. There were saucepans hanging from a rack over the stove, knife blocks, garlic crushers − everything to suggest more than a passing acquaintance with kitchen utensils. In the bathroom there were baskets of shells on gleaming white tiles, in the bedroom everything was colour coordinated. It seemed almost too neat, too clean, at least for any man I'd ever had anything to do with.

It was that night that he told me about Ellen. We were

sitting on his balcony, overlooking the bay below. We talked about this and that, and suddenly, out of the blue, he said: 'I was married you know.'

Caroline was unsure how to deal with this information. She sipped her drink.

'Yes?' she said.

'She died. Last year. In an accident. It was the last thing she did before she died, this flat. She planned it right down to the last detail.'

So there it was, out in the open. And yet in a curious way I did not find it distressing. He was forty-four at the time, nine years older than I was. I'd already wondered why he hadn't mentioned other relationships. It was what, in my experience, people normally did. As we talked, he opened up, he told me more about him and Ellen, that they'd been happily married for seventeen years, that they owned this flat and a farm in the country.

'I was devastated when she died,' he said. 'It's a terrible thing to say but I've actually envied people when I've heard that their partners have died of cancer, or of some lingering illness. I've thought, "Well, at least you had time to say goodbye".' He explained that it was only in the previous month or so that he'd even been able to go out without having to leave early on some pretext, just so he could go home and sit in the dark to think of her. He hadn't visited the farm at all since her death. 'I don't know why I'm telling you all of this,' he said, with a little rueful grin. 'I didn't mean to, it's just that, well . . .' And his voice trailed off. To be honest, I had no idea what to do. In the dark I reached over and squeezed his hand. 'I'm sorry,' I said. But later, back at my hotel, I was not proud of myself for thinking that I was pleased that it was death, not divorce, that meant he was single. It seemed somehow that at least perhaps he might be someone who had the potential to be emotionally available.

As it turned out I couldn't have been more wrong, and I have mostly been alone since my shortlived marriage. Actually, I don't mind most of the time. Juggling motherhood and a career was enough for many years, and neither Harry nor I took kindly to the occasional man-friend who would feel that it was time to rearrange our lives. The closest I have come to anything long term is with another lecturer at the college but in the end he was too dull for me in that tweedy English academic way. And despite having given up my itinerant ways I couldn't quite join him in his slow and careful deliberations about the world at large. Every time I went out with him I felt as though I was in a Malcolm Bradbury novel. Somehow, however, I wasn't surprised when a few years ago he was dismissed for having sex with a student on the desk in his office. Those dull quiet types often seem to hide an incipient sleaziness. (Actually, I felt a pang of envy, I'll admit it. I thought to myself, if he'd had sex with me on his desk, perhaps we might have managed a relationship.) Thank goodness all that stuff has passed me by now, and I don't have to worry anymore.

And now it occurs to me with sudden clarity what the absolute absence of Ellen was: there was not a single photograph in either house. No photographs of anything. You would think as a photographer that perhaps it might have taken me less than twenty years to work it out. But it is only now, writing this, that I can see what was missing so clearly. And even though I am a photographer, and I have documented almost every day of Harry's life (to his chagrin), and there are photographs in our house everywhere, I still think that if I had not been so intent on falling in love, I might have seen in the absence of a photographic record of their lives together, that Paul was not as healed as he seemed, or as I so desperately wished him to be.

I believe it was that night, the night after our almost-row about the sign, that she came and stole him away from me completely. Or to be more precise, he allowed himself to be taken somewhere. After all she was not a malign force, although for many years I have allowed myself to think that it was her spirit wishing him away; but perhaps it was just him, perhaps he saw the swamp and jumped straight into it.

In the night Caroline woke suddenly, jolted out of sleep by the moon shining on her face. Paul sat at an open window, a look of such yearning on his face that it scared her.

'Paul.'

He turned and she reached out a hand to him. Almost as if he was sleepwalking he got into bed, lay down and closed his eyes. She remembered what he'd said on their drive to the farm. 'You can't see your wife like that, at the bottom of a ravine, and not remember it.'

Her sympathetic reply. 'Of course not, I understand.' But now, lying awake beside him, wondering if he was feigning sleep, she realised that this was not how she had imagined it, not how the story of their lives was supposed to be unfolding. Something was going awry and she seemed powerless to stop it.

It was not a good night's sleep. I tossed and turned while Paul slept. In that way of night-time despair I vacillated between doubt and hope. For the first time I thought perhaps I should simply get up and leave – walk out on it all before it got too complicated. And then I would hear my mother's voice telling me over and over that my problem was I was never committed to anybody, that if only I would stick with someone it would be all right. 'Relationships,' she said to me one day, 'are not photographic projects, Caroline,' – and then the inevitable coda – 'whatever your father might think.' But in the end there was this: I had loved him enough to marry him, and he me. Surely, I thought, we can work our way through this. And sometime in the early hours I got up and made myself tea and toast, and it was then that I noticed the woodpile.

I have always loved chopping wood. Ever since I was a child, when my mother first entrusted me with a very small blunt axe, I have understood the inherent beauty of rendering down. When my father left home, I would take the axe and splinter the wood and pretend it was him I was cracking and breaking and splitting into tiny pieces. As an adult I would visit my mother in the country when I was home from assignment, and head happily towards the woodpile. Raising the axe high above my head, and then dropping it so quickly, was almost like an act of atonement – I have been away, I have not been a dutiful daughter, I have missed photographs, yet again I have not found a partner. But now I am back, and from these branches I will create your winter fires for you to sustain you in my absence. I will bring the axe down and as I do each second of failure will be wiped away in a clean, clear movement, and when it's finished I will sigh, and stop, and feel quite empty and still inside.

In the morning when Paul woke, the bed was empty. He stumbled to the kitchen and threw open the back door. Out in the sunshine Caroline was chopping wood, small shards of kindling split and gathered around her. She realised he was there, but she kept on, chopping and chopping, the axe gleaming silver in the sun.

I worked my anger out on the wood. I could feel Paul's eyes on me, but I didn't stop, not until he came right up behind me and touched me. I could sense the desire and pain in him so strongly that all I wanted to do was to turn around and enfold him, wipe away his sadness, comfort him like a child. And so we stood like that, our arms around each other, until he bent to kiss me and at that very moment, he snapped away from me, before I even had a chance to respond.

'I'm sorry, I'm sorry . . . I can't. It's not you . . . it's me. I don't know what's wrong.' Caroline spoke soothingly to him, as she would to a nervous animal, but Paul was backing away from her now, his hands in front of him.

'Why can't you leave me alone?' He roared the words, and they shot like arrows into the air. 'Just leave me alone.'

Chapter FOUR

> Photography records the gamut of feelings
> written on the human face, the beauty of the
> earth and skies that man has inherited . . . It is a
> major force in explaining man to man.
>
> *Edward Steichen*, Time *1961*

My mother died when I was fifty, and I have never felt more acutely my position as an only child, even though I was hardly at an age where you would think I would be dwelling on an ancient vague sense of resentment that my parents hadn't managed to provide me with a sibling before their relationship fell apart. Harry offered to come with me to the cottage – so, in fact did my father – but I felt this was not fair on either of them. My father had not seen her for years, not since Harry's christening – or rather name-giving ceremony – when he was a year old. I felt some strange loyalty to both of them, that he should remember her as she had been then, and that she should not have to suffer the indignity of her ex-husband clearing up an old woman's mess. And I felt equally protective towards Harry. She was seventy-eight when she died, not that old, but she had been infirm for a little while, querulous and distressed after a hip replacement operation which had not quite worked. She had meals on wheels and weekly visits from the district nurse, and my father and I between us paid for a housekeeper, so she was comfortable and even perhaps better looked after than most. When she died the curious thing was that I did not lose my seventy-eight-year-old mother, I lost the mother who had looked after me as a child, and I was stunned by the howling grief that swept over me. She died suddenly – a fall down the stairs in the middle of the night – and I felt guilty about that: we should have put in a StairMaster, we should have had someone with her at night as well as in the day; but in the end I did reason that my mother, always an active woman, at least went quickly. But that of course was reason, which has nothing to do with grief or mourning, although I will say that in the end it helped. And I do not believe that she was taken before her time.

Even in her death it seemed I was protected. By the time I could get there it was twenty-four hours later, time enough for the nurse to have organised a funeral home, and for the housekeeper to have cleaned the house. I did not have to engage with death fully. It was not even as confronting as it had been on occasions when I had been on assignments where, it was understood, although not often stated, death was to be part of the brief. (Newspapers don't actually say, 'Send us back dead bodies, starving children and mayhem', it's just that it's implicit.) I sat with my mother's body for several hours at the funeral home. I talked to her and told her many of the things I had been unable to discuss with her when she was alive – how glad I was that she was such a good grandmother to Harry, how much I appreciated how she had looked after me when I was small, and how much I thanked her for continuing her care of me when my father left, even though we both knew that a large part of her heart died that day and never truly recovered.

As I write these words, two things strike me: how supportive she was when I came back from Australia, and – this is a surprise – how similar our lives have been. We both had extreme careers, she was a speleologist in much the same way I was a photographer, always off exploring some cave or other. Both of us brought up a child alone and compromised our careers in order to do so. And both of us, after the shock of separation from a partner, remained somewhat distanced from relationships. I have spent all my life thinking I was quite different to my mother and now I find I am almost identical. Perhaps when Harry reads these words he will surprise me, perhaps he will say: 'But Mum, you were always like her, I knew that.'

And what of Harry? Will it be the same for him too? Will the events that led up to his birth render him incapable of marriage and a family? If any events were going to affect a child within a womb, what happened to us (because he was there already by then, although I did not know it yet) would surely do it.

All these musings are, I suppose, a way of avoiding the next step. At the time the next step was hard to take as well. I remember that after Paul screamed at me, I went inside. I was too shaken to do anything much, I simply sat at the kitchen table and waited. It wasn't long until he came in. He dropped his hands on my shoulders. 'I'm sorry,' he said. 'I don't know what's wrong.'

It was a fragile peace. They were courteous to one another, almost as if they had only just met.

'Would you like a cup of tea?'

'Thank you.'

Politely dealing with this painful new information.

'I'm sorry,' he said. 'I don't know what came over me.'

'It's all right.' Caroline touched his hand. 'We'll take it easy.'

'Shall we go into Rock Forest?' he said. 'We could look at the church and the museum, have a meal at the pub.'

'That's a nice idea.'

We wandered like tourists around the town. Paul pointed out things he thought I might like to photograph. He was solicitous and quiet. But I was still too distressed to connect with the camera. The camera requires a detached focus, a distillation of subjectivity and objectivity, and every time I lifted it to my eye, it was the sight of Paul backing away from me that I saw, not the landscape in front of me.

If I was to try and explain what Rock Forest was like to a stranger, I would say: imagine Dorset earth transplanted to the Australian bush, imagine a Western ghost town mixed with flashes of European inhabitance – beech trees, the odd Swiss chalet or Scottish hunting lodge next door to leaning shanties made of sheets of tin, gracious oaks next to straggly gum trees, and a few still standing Victorian edifices, most with just their facades complete. And imagine this at the end of the line – a dead-end village in every sense of the word and a feeling of isolation hanging over the emptiness and the dust that coated everything. If you can picture this odd patch-work quilt, and if I tell you that from the first it was considered a painter and photographer's paradise – in fact, curiously enough, I had come quite accidentally to the place that came to house one of the most important photographic records of goldrush life in Australia – then you may just have an inkling of the haunted and haunting nature of this once thriving metropolis.

A few cows and horses wandered the streets, sheltering from the afternoon sun under the tin verandahs.

'It's common ground,' Paul told Caroline.

An old woman wearing several skirts and mismatched shirts came shuffling around a corner, a grey horse on a halter a few steps behind her. The horse was wearing a straw hat with two holes in it for his ears. The woman spotted Paul and Caroline, called out in cheery fashion. 'G'day. Where you been?'

Paul shouted back: 'Been away, Mabel.'

Mabel nodded. 'Hello Ellen,' she called. 'Come 'n' have a yarn, tell us all the news.'

Caroline blanched, but smiled at the crazy old woman. Whispered to Paul: 'Tell her I'm not Ellen.'

Paul looked straight ahead. 'We'll be over soon, Mabel. Don't you worry about that.'

Mabel nodded. 'Don't be a stranger, d'ya hear.' She gave the leading rein a tug. 'C'mon Reverend.'

★

Look, I'll admit it. I can see his point of view about this one. There was no reason why he should try and explain that I was not the person Mabel thought I was. It was only that at the time it seemed like yet another little thing, piled on all the others. And why did she think I was Ellen? It meant I must look more than a little like her. I already knew she was English. What had Paul done, I wondered, married someone as close to the original as possible? Was it his way of pretending none of it had happened? Anyway, I can see now I was being unreasonable, but at the time it didn't feel that way, so I pestered him as we drank our beers in the pub garden in the shade of the trees. I couldn't help myself.

'For god's sake, let it go.' Paul was terse.

'But why didn't you say something? I don't understand.'

'Because she's old and mad. It's a miracle she remembered me, let alone you.'

'But she didn't remember me. She remembered Ellen. That's the point.'

Paul stood up, and slammed down his beer. 'The only point to this conversation is there's no point.'

'Paul!'

So that was it. He disappeared inside the pub and I was left in the garden with my thoughts, and they were not comfortable.

I don't know how long I stayed in the garden. I drank some of my beer, and watched the wasps buzzing around the blossoms. It was quiet and still in the garden, I could easily have stayed there, but I knew already that I'd been wrong, that it was silly to push Paul on something as small as that. What did it matter, after all ... why worry? So I picked up my glass and walked into the darkness of the pub.

Caroline had to blink for her eyes to adjust to the dim light. The hubbub of the pub had disappeared, she realised. Instead there was a strange, almost expectant quiet. Paul was waiting by the bar. Jim was standing a few feet away from him. Everyone, even the pool players, was looking towards the bar, where the barmaid was standing, her arms crossed.

'I told you,' she said, loud and clear. 'I'm not serving no fuckin' murderer.'

Jim's voice was quiet but in the silence of the room Caroline could hear every word.

'And I told you to serve him.'

What hit me at that point was anger. It charged through my body. I was outraged that anybody should say that about Paul, about *my* husband. I walked straight towards him, and stood beside him at the bar, waiting until the barmaid poured us two beers and slammed the glasses down in front of us. Paul drained his in one hit, and put some money down. The men returned to their drinks, to the pool table, to their groups. One of them muttered something, another laughed.

'Thanks.' Paul nodded at Jim and walked out. I stood there for a moment – he hadn't even looked at me – and then followed him into the sunshine. Someone whispered something behind my back. What was it? I strained to hear, until the sound came again, louder, clearer, the barmaid's voice: 'Murderer.' And as I left the echo of the word swelled like a whispering sea behind me. '. . . derer . . . derer . . . erer'.

But just as I was about to swing open the pub door, Jim appeared beside me.

'Can I have a word?' He touched her on the arm and drew her back into the shadow of the pub hallway. 'I'm sorry that happened.'

'Yes.' She wasn't ready to talk to a virtual stranger. She glanced over his shoulder where she could see Paul's car still sitting in the shade. 'Well, why did they say it?'

'I don't know. There've been rumours, that's all. I was going to tell Paul myself, to warn him. We didn't even know he'd remarried until he arrived with you.' He touched her elbow again. 'Anyway,' he said, 'I just wanted to apologise. That barmaid was way out of line.'

Caroline nodded. 'Thanks.' She turned to leave again.

'I might have found a horse for you to try.'

How did he know? How did he pick the one thing that would make me turn around, that would cause me in the midst of this odd scene to smile from ear to ear, to feel genuinely pleased?

'Really?'

'An endurance horse, born and bred in these parts. I hear she's a great little mare. I'll bring her out in a few days if you'd like . . . the owner's moving to the city, wants her to go to a good home.'

'I'd love that. That's kind of you. Thank you.'

He shrugged. 'It's nothing. Happy to help. I'll see you then . . .'

Paul was still waiting for me. He made no mention of the time I'd spent in the pub, and I was in no mood to bring up light conversation, although I must say I wondered about Jim, about his friendship – or lack of it – with Paul. I thought it was kind of him to remember that I liked to ride. It didn't quite fit with his image, somehow, but in comparison to what had happened in the pub, Jim and his place in the scheme of things seemed of little importance. As Paul and I drove in silence back to the farm I thought, 'How can I ask if it is true? Were you her murderer? If you were hers, will you be mine? Have I . . . is it conceivable that I have married a murderer?'

Would I have said the words? I believe I would have, but I had not had time to truly digest the import of what had happened before Paul suddenly put on the brakes and we screeched to a halt. Startled rosellas flung themselves in the air, tiny shards of red and blue breaking against the sky.

Even now I can see those colours. Since I left Australia I have never been back, and yet the colours have haunted me. I have had glimpses of them on holiday with Harry – in Turkey and Greece, in Italy and Spain, in the soft haze of an olive grove, or a clear blue Mediterranean sky – and I have been immediately transported back, back, back. For years I wished I could rewrite it, see what was unfolding in front of me. I suppose it is the feeling every person involved in a preventable tragedy has – if only . . .

★

44

Paul gripped the steering wheel so hard his knuckles were white with rage. He did not – could not? – look at her.

'I did not murder Ellen.'

'No, no of course not.' It was too pat, too quick, she could hear it herself, but he seemed not to notice.

'I don't know why she said it. I don't understand it.' He turned to face her and she could see the pain in his eyes. 'You believe me, don't you?'

What could I say? If I said no, I could be writing my own death warrant, right there and then on that deserted road. If I said yes, just at the moment I would not have been telling the complete truth. In fact the truth had suddenly become obscure to me, as if a cloud had passed across the sun. But I believed him more than I didn't believe him. I truly did not think he was capable of murder, and so I said: 'Yes, of course I believe you.' And my mind said, yes, no, yes, no, yes, no. But he relaxed, his hands dropped off the steering wheel, and he touched my cheek lightly with his fingers.

'It's hard enough, you know,' he said, 'without this.'

I nodded.

'It's hard coming back here. Harder than I thought. We'll come through.'

And he said the words I had been waiting to hear for several days, 'I love you.' But I could feel nothing, nothing at all. I felt all I wanted to do was hide away in the dark somewhere and cry and sleep, and that if I could do that I would wake up fresh and clear in my mind. The sun would come out again.

Chapter FIVE

> The image is always formed by deep structures linked to language as well as to a symbolic organisation of a culture or a society; and that nevertheless the image is also a means of communication and representation of the world which can be found in all human societies. The image is universal, but it is always specific.
>
> *Jacques Aumont,* The Image

I think one of the things that has always impressed me about humanity is its ability to adapt, although often a high price is paid, unnoticed at the time. I've watched children in war zones who have had people killed in front of them, seen their shock and distress, and yet only hours later, with food and rest and comfort, they will play and smile as if their world is magically all right again. I have seen this as subterfuge – the person dying who refuses to believe it – I have seen it in the extraordinary beauty of someone else dying who chooses to make the dying itself a journey of acceptance. We are so versatile, the human race. You do see here, don't you, a certain adaptation? Even now as I write these words, the reader is adapting to them, curious perhaps as to what I may mean. I suppose it is an attempt to explain to myself why I did not just leave Paul and the farm. I believe that by the time we got back to the farm I was already adjusting. I could have left. I should have left, but the new knowledge I had acquired was already some-how being sifted, assimilated, digested. I do not think that I seriously believed that Paul was a murderer, not yet anyway, but I had begun to believe there was a mystery. Yet somehow I had managed to persuade myself – against all evidence to the contrary – that this mystery would not affect me.

When we got back to the farm, we were both quiet. I put the kettle on. He sat down with a book. I think we were too fragile to broach any topic. But as I sat nursing my cup of tea, Paul came into the kitchen.

'Come on,' he said to me. 'I think we should get out of here for a while. Let's go down to the river in the Toyota, take a picnic. We can come back after dark. You'll see everything you've wanted to see. You'll get some great shots.'

And there it was, this dilemma, staring me right in the face. How could I say: But what happens if you murder me down there? What will you say? Will it look like an accident? Will you bury me, pretend I've left suddenly, gone back to Sydney or England? I couldn't. For some reason I couldn't even bring myself to say: But why now? Let's recover from this. Let's do it tomorrow. And so I did not answer, I simply sat at the kitchen table, until Paul laughed. 'What on earth are you thinking?' he said, cheer-fully, naturally. 'That I'm going to murder you and bury the evidence? Don't you feel safe with me?' And he dropped a kiss on my head. 'Come on,' he said. 'You'll love it,' and he began to whistle as he loaded provisions into a box. 'Baked beans, sausages, potatoes, a bottle of red, tomato sauce.' And so he went on, and he was so ... so normal that I thought, Well, what the hell − let's go. It couldn't be worse, it seemed to me, than sitting in a house which was gaining daily in ghosts and memories and menace.

The idea of territory has been somewhat on my mind of late. The reason being that I have been having a few argu-ments with both the head of the arts faculty at college, and another lecturer, another photographer who was employed a year or so ago. I have not had much to do with him − to tell the truth I try and avoid college life as much as I can outside of working hours − but I have been increasingly distressed at the way he appears to have set himself up in competition to me. He seems almost to be trying to woo students away from my classes to his − he has been running photographic quiz nights with prizes, taking groups of stu-dents out for wine nights, or to cheap restaurants, starting his classes with warm-up periods which seem to consist of making a huge amount of noise, and since his classroom is next to mine, I find it very disturbing.

I spoke to John, the head of the faculty, about it and he was friendly, but at the same time not exactly sympathetic. 'Look, Caroline,' he said, 'You've been here a long time. You're a good teacher, and you get great results, surely there's room for two different styles?' But still, the next time I saw Luke in the corridor I asked him to keep the noise down a bit. We'd met of course, in the staffroom, and at the occasional staff or arts faculty meeting. Somebody told me he used to be a fashion photographer, which only increased my distrust. Anyway, when I asked him, he was easygoing about it. (Much more easygoing, I feel compelled to admit, than I would have been if someone had criticised my teaching methods.) 'Sure,' he said, 'no problem.'

I thanked him and that was that, we went our separate ways, but for a brief moment I felt dissatisfied, as if I had been expecting him to disagree with me. That night I dreamt I was trying to have an argument with a man who simply wouldn't argue with me – it wasn't him, it was no-one I knew. I became so frustrated and angry that in the end I produced a knife and began to stab him, but still he wouldn't argue, he simply sat there and bled in front of me. At this time I have nothing to say about this, or at least nothing I want to say.

However, I will mention something which may or may not be related, and that is a state that I call being on red alert. It is a very uncomfortable state and one to which I am unfortunately accustomed. It began for me when I was eight, when my father upped and left. I mean, one day he was there, and the next he wasn't. There was no explanation from my mother or from him, ever. I was simply required to adjust. And in the same way that I was speaking of those children in war zones, I suppose I did. I went to school, I played, I had friends, I rode my pony, but something had been triggered within me – a state of deep distrust and a suspicion that if I took my eye off the ball, anybody's ball, something disastrous or catastrophic might happen. Perhaps if this had not been compounded by what happened to me in Australia, perhaps I might have learnt to live with it, or even survive it, but as it was it has become part of my life. So now, despite John's assurances that everything was fine with my teaching, I have been left on red alert. My reading of what he said to me is that I am old ('been here a long time'), passé ('everybody has a right to try new things'), and about to be discarded. I know that I am taking this too far, but I am unable to help myself. So at the same time that I am trying to relive a past nightmare I am creating a present one.

(I begin to wonder how I could ever show this to Harry. What would he make of *this* mother, who is beginning to appear to me as a writhing mess of insecurities?)

Acutally, I say that I have had arguments with Luke, and that is not strictly true. It is more as my dream suggests, that I would like to argue with him, but other than the sheer volume of noise erupting from his classroom I can't actually pin him down with anything specific. And when he passes me, or sees me in the common room, he always smiles in a friendly way which I dislike intensely. I take as little notice of him as possible. He also appears to be teaching his students a minimum of theory, which I simply cannot condone. It is one thing for them to discard it once they have taken it on board, quite another not to know it in the first place. Ruskin, Lacan, the Klein Group, Breton, Duchamp, Barthes – these are only a few of the names with which they should be familiar. They should understand how and why these people have tried to understand the art of seeing, as Berger would have it, or even the science of seeing, what John Ruskin called 'a science of the aspect of things'. Also, some of these students of ours will not become photographers, and they need to be equipped to become other things – curators, administrators, lecturers – if they so desire.

I read back through these words and am startled to find that they resemble an elderly person's rant. And that's another thing about Luke. I can't quite tell how old he is. He seems to be of my vintage, and yet he behaves like somebody much younger, and I disapprove of that as well. Does all this make me a fuddy-duddy? That's what Harry calls me every now and then. 'You're a darling old fuddy-duddy,' he says cheerfully when I try to remonstrate about a habit of his. It never upsets me too much. I've kept myself quite well, I know that. I exercise, I eat well, I don't smoke or drink, I've even given up coffee. I wear clothes which I hope are fashionable without being too trendy, although I must say I have a fear of suddenly appearing as mutton dressed as lamb. In fact I have a pact with Harry that he will tell me if he ever sees me in anything that makes me look ridiculous. What I can't help is my face, which tells me every time I look in the mirror that I am in my fifties when inside I still feel, I don't know, thirty-five at the most.

In the meantime however, getting back to photography in general, it is my belief that students must learn to take photographs wherever they are, whatever they are doing. Sorting through my photographs I am reminded of the occasions with Paul when for one reason or another I did not take photographs, and now, even all these years later, how I wish I had.

★

The track was bumpier and the descent more perilous and steeper than anything Caroline had ever experienced in her life. She held on for grim death while Paul pointed out landmarks or kangaroos that seemed to disappear mysteriously the moment she looked in their direction.

'I wish you'd keep two hands on the steering wheel.' She was quickly becoming convinced that both of them were more likely to die from misadventure than from any murderous plan on his part.

But Paul was unconcerned. 'I know this track like the back of my hand.' And gradually, she couldn't help herself, she began to thaw towards him.

I'll tell you how bumpy and steep it was – I didn't even want to get my camera out. I just wanted to get down there. To reach the river. To stop. And so I have no photos I can show you of the way down, nothing that says I travelled this track sitting beside the husband who may or may not have murdered his first wife.

The river. That shining silver thread from the top of the hill was now a foaming, frothing mass, tumbling over rocks, splashing into pools, snaking its way through the valley. Paul bumped over flat river stones until he came to a natural swimming hole, a huge rockface protecting it on one side, a wide sandy bank on the other.

'Our very own beach,' he said, spreading a blanket on the sand and unpacking the basket. 'Let's get some wood.'

Caroline stretched her arms towards the sky. 'It's like standing in the middle of a Beethoven symphony.'

Imagine what I could have photographed, if I hadn't been quite so caught up in my own life! You would not have found pastoral picture postcards in that lot. No, this was Weston country on another continent, where texture is crucial, or Carleton Watkins with his devotion to space, which of course is the reverse of emptiness. Not that I have ever quite reached that league – apart from once or twice, by accident – but it does surprise me how minutely I can recall that landscape all these years later. It seems that even when I was not using my camera, my brain was photographing these surroundings. I remember every thistle, every piece of mistletoe, every blackberry bush and prickly pear – any colour that stood out against that wonderful olive grey blanket covering those rounded hills. I drank it all in, every little bit of it, while Paul and I busied ourselves with the fire. And later, when the fire was flickering steadily and the potatoes were on, Paul suggested a swim.

'You must be mad!' But no, he meant it, indeed he was already stripping off.

Caroline couldn't resist watching him – he seemed so natural, so unconcerned, as if the events of the last few days were forgotten.

'Come on,' he said. 'Last one in is a rotten egg.'

And as he raced towards the water, she too began to undress, but unlike him she felt embarrassed by her nakedness in front of this man who had spurned her so completely only that morning. She got out of her clothes coyly,

53

like a little girl in front of strangers, and walked slowly to the water's edge.

'It's lovely.' Paul surfaced. 'Hardly cold at all.'

She put a foot in and gasped. 'My God. You liar. It's freezing.'

He laughed. 'You're the one who grew up in England.' And he dived under again, while she wobbled her way in on the river stones until they gave way to flatter gravel, covered in weed. It was murky. She wasn't even sure she wanted to go right under. Up to her waist in it, her nipples ached with cold, and she clasped her arms to stop herself from shivering. A flicker of colour caught her eye. On the one rock that was still left in sunlight was a snake. 'Look!' she shouted to Paul.

He stood up and followed her pointing finger. 'It's a red-bellied black. It won't hurt you. It'll disappear now we've disturbed it.'

But as he said the words, the snake slithered from the rock into the water and began swimming straight towards her.

It began to swim straight towards me. Can you imagine that? I threshed in the water and turned to try and run out but Paul called out from the other side of the swimming hole.

'Stand still, for Christ's sake stand still.'

And somehow I could sense the urgency in his voice, so I did. I stood completely still. My arms dropped down by my sides, while the snake slowly, almost gracefully, its head raised out of the water, swam so close to me I could easily have reached out and touched it. If I had wanted. I could see its scales, I could see its eyes, and the occasional flicker of red as its body undulated in the water. And when

it had passed me, I turned and watched its stately progression to the far edge of the pool, until it swam out onto the sandy bank and disappeared.

Caroline stood there, freezing and stunned. As Paul reached her, put his arms around her, the tears began to fall.

'There there,' he soothed her, wiped her eyes with his hand, held her close to his chest, both of them in the murky river water. 'It's all right'. He guided her out of the water, put towels around her, sat her by the fire while she cried. 'It wouldn't have wanted to hurt you,' he said. 'It wasn't looking for you.'

And I couldn't even say, but that is only a tiny bit of why I'm crying. I'm crying for everything, for you and for me, for Ellen, for everything that existed between us a week ago and is gone now. I am crying from confusion and from the certain knowledge that somehow our lives are changing and we are almost powerless to stop it. (Actually I don't think I was quite that prescient, but that was the gist of it, and it was the gist of what I was unable to say.) But he soothed me and cuddled me, and gradually I felt more normal. We got dressed and poured ourselves a beaker of wine and Paul gave me a hearty plate of blackened food, which, despite the charcoal content tasted delicious.

I was beginning to wonder if Australia had a personal vendetta against me.

'I don't think Australia likes me much,' I said, staring into the flames, and Paul laughed.

'Australia's full of creepy crawlies, or do they forget to put that in the travel brochures? Anyway,' he said, 'if you were with Aborigines, they would be telling you how lucky you'd been. The snake would be your totem now. They'd think you were luckier still if it had bitten you. If you survived, of course.'

Was he serious? He probably was. I didn't think of it as lucky at the time. Although I had reason to be more than a little grateful to a snake only a few days later.

Lying back beside Paul, Caroline allowed herself to feel keen pleasure for the mere fact that she was alive. Her nerve ends tingled from the drive, the swim, her close escape. Her whole body felt loose and contented. As the evening closed in around them a small group of wallabies made their way to the water to drink.

She leant over to Paul and kissed him on the lips, and for a moment he responded, pulling her down to him, his tongue urgent inside her mouth. And then just as suddenly he sat up.

'I can't. I'm sorry.' He stood up and looked away from her, as if she was ... what? Something dirty, disgusting.

'Why not?'

He picked up a flat pebble, skimmed it across the surface of the water. 'I don't know. I just can't.' He turned to her, that look again on his face. 'Do you mind? Can you wait?'

With more optimism than she felt she said, 'I'll try.'

'Thank you.' He looked up at the sky. 'We'd better be heading back. I don't want to be driving up the hill in the dark.'

And while they packed, while they got ready, all the time she was wondering if she could spend her life married to someone who couldn't bear to touch her.

★

Too right that's what I was thinking at the time.

But god, it stirs things in me, writing this. Not for Paul. Too much water under the bridge and too long ago. It occurs to me that I have almost forgotten what it feels like to be sexually alive. I gave up masturbating at the same time that I had my menopause. I really didn't feel like it. I think I've put any sexual energy I used to have into my filing system. For the first time in years I wish that I was not so old, so set in my ways. It would be nice to fuck someone even if that's all it was. But I would have no idea how to go about it. (I think this is a temporary aberration, and this paragraph must certainly be deleted.)

Back at the house Caroline made tea and toast. They chatted, sat and read their books. Paul stretched, yawned, stood up.

'Well,' he said, 'I think I'll turn in.'

Caroline was ready to be generous. At least she was fairly sure she was not about to go to bed with a murderer.

'Good idea,' she said. 'I'll join you.'

'Do you mind?' His voice sounded high, strained. He spoke too quickly. 'I think I might sleep in the spare room. I haven't been sleeping too well. I thought it might be better, if you don't mind.'

I shrank back as if he'd scalded me. 'Of course,' I said. 'Yes, of course. That's fine by me. You get a good night's sleep.'

'Thank you.' He patted my shoulder. 'I knew you'd understand.'

★

In the night she had such dreams, such tossing, anxious hot dreams. She dreamt someone was standing over her. He was holding a heavy object above her head. She tried to scream, but no noise came.

'Caroline! Wake up!' Paul's voice was insistent. Urgent. She dragged herself awake, up from the depths. He was standing by the bed.

'You were having a nightmare. You were calling out.'

'God!' She sat up. 'I dreamt someone was trying to ... was trying to ...'

'What?'

'Trying to break in. That's all. Someone was trying to break in.'

He sat on the side of the bed. 'Are you okay now?'

'Yes, yes. I'm fine.'

'Would you like me to, well ...' He looked at his side of the bed.

'No.' She couldn't bear the thought of him next to her if it wasn't where he wanted to be. 'That's okay. I'm fine.'

'All right then.' He went towards the door. As he reached it, she wished she could stop him.

'Paul?'

'Yes?'

'Nothing. Don't worry. Nothing.'

He shrugged and left.

As Caroline settled herself back in the bed she noticed the bed light, a kitsch fifties lamp, a black boy holding a spear, the lightshade balanced on his other arm. She picked it up and held it in her hand. It fitted snugly. A perfect weapon.

I wonder what I meant by that? Did I mean that it was a perfect weapon for me in order to protect myself, or did I mean that Paul had been standing over me, that he intended to hurt me, that I woke by mistake, and that he, having misjudged it, had to pretend he was waking me? But I have to say that even if that was what I thought at the time, it was far-fetched. There are easier ways to kill your wife than with a sidelight, after all.

Chapter SIX

It was in 1931 that Walter Harryjamin first used
the term 'optical unconscious'. 'We have no
idea at all,' he said, 'what happens during the
fraction of a second when a person steps out.'
He goes on to say that photography, 'with its
devices of slow motion and enlargement, reveals
the secret. It is through photography that we
first discover the existence of this optical
unconscious, just as we discover the instinctual
unconscious through psychoanalysis.' Write an
essay describing what you believe the purpose
of photography to be, and how it connects with
the optical unconscious.

CS: questions for second-year students

Do I agree with Harryjamin? Up to a point, but I
wonder – what about the world we see around us?
Hills, fields, cities even – do they have an unconscious? I

think I would argue strongly that they do. That they, as much as any human, are a product of everything that has gone before, and that their collective information lies within something which we may as well call their unconscious. (It just occurs to me that what I am really saying here is that I hope nature has a filing system!)

One thing where I think I have been very lucky in my life is that while my romantic relationships could best be described as absent, I have had many friendships with young people and particularly with young men. I found it refreshing to bring up a boy with the constant level of physical activity, the wrestling and tumbling and play-fighting, none of it familiar from my somewhat lonely childhood. I liked having Harry's friends around. It gave me the feeling of a larger family. They would stay and eat us out of house and home, sleep the night and leave a trail of devastation wherever they went, but I enjoyed it. I found that all of them liked to chat, all of them liked to be mothered, just a little bit. As Harry grew up I noticed that some of his friends would drop by for a coffee even if he was not there. (Did it ever cross my mind? Just once. Although it was not my idea, it was his. He surprised me, ran his hand down my spine while I was reaching for a coffee cup. I turned, and he would have kissed me, but I pushed him away. 'Why not?' he said. I was outraged: 'I've known you since you were eight!' He shrugged. 'I don't see what difference that makes.' If he'd had the words of an older man, he might have managed it, but they were a teenager's words. He didn't drop by much after that and I realised that I missed his company.)

Teenagers, children too, like photography. I think one of the best presents you can give a visual child is a polaroid camera – even these days with CD-ROMS and digital cameras, there is still nothing that compares to taking a photograph and seeing it appear like magic. It's what I gave Harry. He's moved on of course, he's studying film. He wants to be director or a cinematographer. I don't blame him. If the opportunities had existed when I was younger I would probably be intrigued by film. As it is I enjoy it but I find it almost always disappointing. Film acts like a smorgasbord on the senses – too much, or too little, or not the right mix. A fine photograph can be stared at for hours; it will only gradually reveal its secrets. Also I find the arrogance of directors somewhat disturbing. I remember reading an interview with George Miller when he made *The Witches of Eastwick*. Comparing the film to Updike's book, he said, 'I prefer my version.' His *version*? Excuse me? In this case, this is no chicken and egg situation. The book came first. The book is *the* version. Updike was *the* creator. (No matter what you think of the book – or the film – that is immaterial. The fact is without the book there would have been no film.) Harry, full of theory and youth and testosterone, disagrees. 'The director's vision – and that's really what Miller meant, Mum,' he says, 'the director's vision is absolute on a film, and it is his vision, no matter where it came from.' 'Or hers,' I generally say at this point in what is a fairly frequent argument. 'Or hers,' he concedes. But I am not persuaded and never will be.

I've often used my relationship with Harry as a kind of blueprint for my relationship with my students – minus the obvious lifelong bond, of course – so whilst I've always had a 'proper' relationship with my students, I've also always prided myself on the fact that I am there for them if they need me. I like to feel that they can come and talk about their work, or lives, or pretend to talk about their work in order to talk about their lives and they will find me approachable and supportive. And more or less I think this has been the case.

Which brings me back to the question of Luke, who has quite definitely become some sort of question. Just as I was locking up my room this evening he materialised beside me.

'I was wondering if you'd like to meet me for a coffee?'

It was very abrupt, and a look of amazement must have crossed my face because he added quickly: 'I need to talk to you about Lisa.' Now Lisa is one of my more troubled students, but she is one of mine, not his, so boundaries were being crossed. But we were there in a public place, surrounded by people, and he was urgent about it. 'It's important,' he said.

'We can meet in my office or in the staffroom . . .'

But he shook his head. 'I'd rather not if you didn't mind.'

I shrugged. 'Okay. I guess so.'

So we made a time for tomorrow to meet at a nearby coffee shop. And that is all really, but I can't help wondering in my increasingly red alert state, What does he know about Lisa that I don't? Why does he want to see me? I almost rang her tonight, but felt I might be breaking a confidence.

Harry noticed that I was distracted. These nights I can't wait to open up the computer and begin typing. (I have a terrible feeling it's becoming a kind of therapy, something I avoided even when my mother was trying to force me to contact Paul, to let him know that he had a child. She tried to enlist the help of a psychiatrist friend of hers, but to no avail. I have never seen why I should introduce Harry to that can of worms.)

'I don't know what you're doing in there night after night, but you don't seem very happy,' he said to me, while we ate our dinner.

'It's just a project I've got an idea for . . . that's all.'

'Well, don't let it get to you. You should go out more,' he said, flinging the dishes – unrinsed of course – into the dishwasher. And he was off, stripping off his clothes as he headed for the bath and his aftershave and clean black clothes; out into the night to meet Karen, while I sat alone in the dark, the screen my company, the ever increasing pressure of the memories saying, choose me, choose me.

By the morning Caroline had come to her conclusions.

'We can't go on like this,' she said, when they were seated at the breakfast table.

'Like what?'

'All this.' She waved a hand around the room. 'Going on with all these normal things as if what is happening here is normal. It's not. I've never lived like this before. I think we should go back to Sydney before it's too late.'

'No.' Paul's face contorted. 'I thought you liked it here.'

'It's hard to like a place when it's set against you. My god, Paul, we've only been here a few days and look what's happened to us . . .'

'You're taking it too seriously.' He got up and began to pile the dishes. 'Look, it's all explainable and the snake, well, that was unusual but there are hundreds of snakes here, it's not that surprising.'

'I'm not talking about the snake.' She paused a moment. 'I'm talking about Ellen. It's because of her that you don't want to touch me, isn't it? That's why you don't want to leave.'

'That's not true. It's you I love. I just need a bit more time, that's all, just give me a bit more time.'

He picked up her hand and kissed it. 'It'll be all right.'

And as I sat there and pondered this strange turn of events and whether I should stand by what I had said, there was a sudden commotion outside. A horse neighed, a dog barked. There was a sound of hooves and a male voice shouting out.

'Cooee, anyone home? Jeezus! Bloody dog. Anyone home?'

Outside Jim was on a horse and leading another. Riding a bay and leading a chestnut, already saddled and bridled.

Caroline breathed her pleasure into the air. 'She's beautiful.'

'Isn't she though?' Jim looked pleased as punch, as if he himself were responsible for the mare's existence. 'She's the one I told you about. Born and bred in this country but the owner wants out. Do you want to try her out?'

'I'd love to. I'll get my boots.'

I wish I knew what Jim and Paul said to each other while I was inside. I could hear the rise and fall of their voices.

What would it have been about? About the day before in the pub? Did they voice their mutual suspicion of one another? I don't think it went that far, but something happened because when I went out, Paul simply turned on his heel and walked inside. Perhaps, if there hadn't been a horse involved, I might have followed him, but as it was I hardly noticed. I patted the mare and mounted. I looked across at Jim.

'What's wrong with Paul?'

He shrugged. 'Search me.'

'Never mind.' The mare was frisky, keen to be on the move. 'Let's go.'

I don't ride much these days. It's a sorrow to me, but it's the price I paid for choosing to live in London. Well, it was not much choice really. I lived with my mother for two years while Harry was a baby, and travelled backwards and forwards to Oxford to do relief teaching or casual teaching, or the odd assignment that wouldn't take me too far from home. Then I was offered the job at the college. It was too good an opportunity to turn down. A regular income, the chance to get a flat. We rented for a while and then managed to buy this one in Battersea not far from the college, a short walk to the park. The park and the ponds had to replace the river and fields. It has never been quite the same but at least they are something. For a while I tried to ride every now and then, but I would get out of condition and then push myself too hard. On one weekend in the country I fell off over a jump and tore all the ligaments in my shoulder. My mother was furious.

'I can't believe you could be that irresponsible,' she said to me while she filled me with painkillers and called the doctor to see if I was concussed. 'You've got a job and a child now. How could you jeopardise yourself like that?'

For the first time in my life I had to agree. I hated agreeing. I hated to think that I had to curtail my own activities because of this small extension of myself that seemed to be occupied with subsuming me. Or because I now had to turn up to work nine to five, and what use would a paraplegic lecturer be? – as my mother so swiftly (but in fact incorrectly although I knew what she meant) pointed out.

But she was right and so I have learnt to live without riding, but it's not been easy. Horses were my way out of dealing with life when I was a child, despite the extreme reality of their natures. My pony, for instance, used to fart in my face every time I cleaned out her back hooves. Hardly romantic. And why do children who would never clean up their bedrooms cheerily clean out stables full of smelly manure? All I know is that there have been certain times when I've been riding when it's as if, just for a moment, you and the horse are more than the sum of your parts. There is a transition in a gallop, for instance, where suddenly it moves from being merely fast to being swift, as if every sense is increased a hundredfold.

You know what I dread? I dread becoming old and dying without once again feeling that feeling. And yet it is so far removed from my life now that it is hard to see how I can ever recapture it. I think it may be the only thing I am truly nostalgic for.

★

Caroline couldn't help fidgeting in the unfamiliar stock saddle.

Jim looked over at her. 'You've got to ride like a cowboy, legs long and forward. None of this upright English stuff. Slouch a bit. You'll be right.'

She tried it, and was suddenly on an armchair. The mare picked her way carefully between the rocks, and as they rode along the ridge line they could see the valley several miles below them. Caroline inhaled the smell of warm horse in the sunshine. She ran her fingers through the mare's mane.

'What's her name?' she called.

'Belle.'

'Belle. Come on then, Belle.'

I remember that ride as if it was yesterday. Everything about that time is still crystal clear, and that ride – if I close my eyes I am back there instantly. It was a perfect day for riding, a blue, blue sky, a slight chill in the air. A wedge-tailed eagle circled above us. I saw it all with a stranger's eyes. It seemed to me that the whole landscape was trying to camouflage itself; the lichen covering rocks to be the same colour as the whispering tips of the gum trees, the green grey pastel landscape hiding vermilion parrots, chocolate coloured wallabies. We saw snakes, and I couldn't help but shudder, although they slid quickly away. When we reached a plateau we galloped for a while, and I could feel Belle sure-footed beneath me. When we pulled up, Jim fished in his pocket and lit up a cigarette.

'When I'm up here it seems to me I could step off one

of these hills and be swallowed up,' he said, looking down towards the river.

I nodded. I could still remember the sensation of wanting to jump into the arms of the early morning fog.

And then he quoted me this poem. I have it still. It is by Rilke. I could not remember it word for word after all these years. I might not have remembered it at all if it hadn't been for the fact that Harry had studied this same poem at school; and although I felt that between the first time I had heard it and all that time later, it had been debased for me, the fact was that when I heard Jim speak it, it was pure. At that time it was pure. It went like this:

What birds plunge through is not the intimate space
in which you see all forms intensified.
(Out in the Open, you would be denied
your self, would disappear into that vastness.)
Space reaches *from* us and construes the world:
to know a tree, in its true element,
throw inner space around it, from that pure
abundance in you. Surround it with restraint.
It has no limits. Not till it is held
in your renouncing is it truly there . . .

I have to say I was impressed. I was not attracted to Jim, or not obviously so, but it was a bit like the Marlboro man suddenly quoting James Joyce.

'That's just right . . . that's exactly right,' I said to him.
'I thought you'd know it, being English and all that.'
I told him: 'I've never been much of a one for poetry.'
'What a shame . . . not to be much of a one for poetry.'

69

I was confused. 'Well, you don't seem, I mean, you're not the poetic type yourself really, are you?'

' "And is there honey still for tea?" All that jazz. Ah well, it's the Irish in us Australians, you see. You can't have Irish blood and not love language. Words, women and whisky ... that's what my Da passed on to me, even though he'd never set foot in the auld country either. It was his parents that came out here.'

We started walking again, side by side down the dirt track.

'How did you end up here then?' I was curious now about him. He seemed even more of an unlikely official than before.

'I was looking for a place to run and hide, I guess. I was in Vietnam, it took a toll. I came up here with a mate in the early seventies to pan for gold. He left. I stayed. After I'd settled a few fights in the pub by clobbering everybody around me, the parks department suggested I put my soldiering to good use and become their boundary rider, I suppose. Make sure nobody did the wrong thing in the National Parks. Keep an eye out on the tourists. The locals hated me at first, of course. I used to think they'd shoot me soon as look at me, but I don't know ... we got used to each other somewhere along the way.' His voice trailed away.

His voice trailed away because of the question that Caroline had to ask him. The one question she had not asked him since they had started their ride, the one hanging over both of them. He knew it was coming. How could he not?

'Jim?'

She saw him tense slightly on his horse, his gaze straight down towards the river.

'Yes?'

She almost whispered the words, almost hoped he wouldn't catch them, that they too could be swallowed up into the air.

'Did he kill her?'

Did he hear her? He gazed ahead. He gathered his reins in one hand, and his free hand went into his jacket pocket to pull out a cigarette. He did not look at her, not once.

'He helped.'

Chapter SEVEN

> You can strengthen a composition by choosing
> your emphasis. Underexposure of the fore-
> ground for instance, and of the mid-distance,
> will concentrate the effect of the background.
> This is a good way to photograph mountain
> scenery. A shallow depth of field will emphasise
> the foreground. Don't forget that if you are
> shooting animals, working close up greatly
> reduces depth of field. Selective focusing will
> separate the animal from the background.
>
> *CS: notes to students for Lake District*
> *field trip 1993*

If I had been less preoccupied with what it is I am writing, I might have lent more thought to why exactly Luke would want to talk to me about Lisa. There are several things, in fact, that I should have been lending some thought to. My father, for one. My child for another.

However, if I had thought about it, had tried to prepare myself in advance, I don't suppose I would have come anywhere near the truth.

When we met at the coffee shop, I was distracted. I arrived with too many bags of shopping, seduced, as always, by Safeway specials, and I felt dishevelled and out of sorts. A feeling not helped by Luke's late arrival. It was not an auspicious beginning.

I begin to be unsure how to approach this. The fact is, I am furious. Present and past fury seem to be on a collision course. I have to explain the level of fury I experienced when Jim had finished filling me in on the details he felt I was missing about Ellen's death, and life. But I also wish to vent my spleen about Luke, because of how our conversation made me feel. Which was belittled, old and furious. But I find it hard to write, so I said, so he said. I have the sense that these furies are connected, that perhaps they go even deeper. Perhaps I am also furious with my father, with my child ... which begs the question, And with myself? But why with myself? What have I done? *I* am not at fault here.

I can say these are the facts, I can explain the setting, but somehow this is not enough. I want to describe the picture, I want to describe the woman in the picture, the man in the picture. The woman waiting at the table, increasingly agitated, for the man to arrive to explain why he wanted to see her.

Actually, this bothers me too, this desire to write about myself as not-myself. Surely at my age I can describe a personal event without having to resort to the pretence that I am someone else? And yet how else do I explain how it came about, or hazard a guess at Luke's thoughts? What I have learnt is that if something affects me, I immediately see it as a documentary photograph. It is a way to distance myself from the emotions involved. It goes into black and white, it becomes a scene I look at. It is me-not-me in there. I am the woman, Luke is the man, we are in a café. It is a cold grey day, a typical day in London. The man, he is grey-haired, tall, probably in his early fifties, he is wearing a long black overcoat against the chill. If the person waiting for him did not dislike him, she would probably describe him as attractive.

It is the kind of day Sergio Larrain photographed all those years ago, visiting London with his Chilean background, all that sunshine and colour. He must have been amazed by the pervading gloom of London because he caught the fog, the queues, that grey, that sense of history underneath the streets waiting to seize you and drag you underground in a way no British photographer has ever quite managed. The kind of day in which you've been told by your father's partner that despite what he says, he is not okay, that he may not be okay again. Which is to say, he might die. The kind of day in which she suggests you'd better visit soon with his grandson, and you are not happy about any of this: the meeting, the delay, the weather, the price of shopping, your hair, which is having a bad day, your father . . . your life. (And there is something else too, something your father has told your son, which you do not know yet.)

When the man arrived, he was flustered.

'I'm sorry,' he said. 'The bus was late. What to do?' He shrugged.

She felt like saying, Catch an earlier bus, perhaps, but bit her tongue. She was already halfway through her second coffee and feeling nervy.

'You wanted to see me?'

She sounded terse, she knew it. She didn't care.

The man said, 'Cut to the chase, eh? No polite chitchat. All right, fine. Well, as you know, I wanted to talk to you about Lisa.'

Oh yes indeedy. He certainly did. He certainly wanted to talk about Lisa. At first the woman thought it was probably because he was having an affair with her, although why he would confide that information to a fellow teacher she was not sure. But no, it transpired that the manner in which he wanted to talk about her was twofold. Namely that this Lisa had a) developed some kind of unrequited passion for him and he wanted the woman's advice, because, he said, the woman was old enough to be Lisa's mother, and he had heard she was a mother and therefore he thought she might be able to help him; and b) this Lisa was complaining to him about her, the woman, her teaching methods and her manner of disciplining her students and the amount of work she set them and she wanted to swap to the man's course, which the man didn't want because of a).

And this was when the woman felt this cold fury building up in her and she said to the man: 'So you thought you could tell me all this and because I am old enough to be her mother, I would advise you about this predicament, and at the same time not be offended by all this crap she's been spinning you about my classes?'

The man nodded and said, Yes, he didn't know where to turn or what to do and he had thought that she would understand.

Very carefully the woman picked up her coffee and threw it over him and walked outside.

The man followed her down the street while she stomped along with her bags of shopping, and he kept saying, 'What did I say? What did I do? You could at least stop and talk to me.'

But she just kept right on walking, and in the end he fell back. She felt him stand and watch her and she just kept on walking.

So that is the story of my morning. This evening there was a message on my machine from Luke. He was apologetic. Would I please ring him? I erased it. Not a chance, I said. Not a chance.

But why exactly am I so adamant about it? After all, I *am* old enough to be Lisa's mother. I know that, so why should it bother me? And she has always been a troublesome student, or should I say, a troubled student. It somehow doesn't surprise me that she is pursuing him. He is not unattractive, even if he is not my type. I feel adamant because goddamn it, this is what teaching is all about. This is his problem, not mine. It only becomes mine if she lodges an official complaint against me, or if she asks to leave my class. Why should I help him solve his problem?

I was adamant when I got back from the ride with Jim, too. I didn't tell him what I was thinking. We rode along and chatted inconsequentially about this and that. He left the mare with me. 'Keep her a few days, try her out.'

When I went into the house I felt that fury rise in me.

The same one as this morning, the one that will brook no opposition. I walked into the bedroom and began to fling my clothes into the suitcase. Paul followed me of course.

'What did that shit say to you? Did he tell you I killed her? Did he? Jesus, Caroline, did he?' He moved towards her, and she recoiled.

'Leave me alone.'

She began to pack her spongebag, her book from beside the table, the little things, the last things. She could feel all the distress of the last few days fall away. It was as if a cloud had lifted.

'You could at least tell me why.'

She closed the clasps, put the case on the floor, straightened her hair.

'Because you are a liar.'

'What?' His voice. She must not be taken in by his voice. 'Christ, Caroline, I've never lied to you.'

And I looked my husband straight in the eyes and said, 'Oh yes you have. Let me see: You told me you and Ellen were happy, and you weren't, you weren't happy at all. You told me you'd warned her about the brakes and Jim says you didn't. You didn't tell me she was English, you didn't tell me she looks, I mean looked, like me ... what more can I say? Is there anything I've missed, or is that it?'

He grabbed my arm. 'Did he say I killed her?'

I paused for a second. 'He said you helped.'

For a moment I thought he might actually strike me. He raised his hand above his head, and then it was as if all the fight went out of him, almost as if he had been deflated. He sat on the bed and watched me.

'How are you thinking of going, just as a matter of interest? Were you going to leave me without a car? Steal the Toyota perhaps?'

There is a clue in there isn't there? To me, I mean, rather than the story. Because the fact of the matter is that I had given it no thought at all. I was simply going to walk away. I didn't want to hear his side of the story. I'd had it. I was, as they say these days, out of there, although even hiking my suitcase up to the road would have taken some doing. But now I see this: it is not unusual for me to react like this. In fact I have already done it twice today. This morning with Luke, this evening with Harry. Three times if you count my telling of the story. So I stood there, and I was mystified, I have to admit. I did not know what to say. Perhaps if I had worked things through a little more carefully, I might have got out of the house there and then. But Paul laughed, and somehow the laughter cracked my anger.

'You're a goose,' he said. 'You really are. And you look most uncomfortable standing there like that.'

It was hard to remain on my dignity with someone laughing at me. So I sat down on the bed as well, and he put his hand over mine.

'Look,' he said, 'I'm not going to murder you. I didn't murder Ellen. I loved her. I want you to come with me . . . I want to show you something, and when I have, if you still want to leave, well, I'll drive you into Bathurst myself. I'll drive you back to Sydney if that's what you want. Okay?'

What choice did I have? He seemed so sane at that moment. And the truth was still that he had made no attempt to hurt me, none whatsoever. But also I thought, well, if we were off the property it would be easier to make a run for it if I needed to. Plus I was curious as well. I wondered what he could possibly want to show me that might make a difference to this strange impasse we found ourselves in.

It wasn't until they were driving along beside the river that Caroline realised they were on the bridle track, and almost as soon as the realisation hit her Paul slammed on the brakes.

'My god!'

He climbed out of the Toyota. 'A blue-tongue,' he said.

She watched while he gently lifted the lizard off the road and into the scrub nearby. It seemed unlikely behaviour for a killer, but even so she hastily scanned the truck for – for what? Something to protect herself should the need arise. In the glovebox she found a Swiss army knife, and she slipped it into the pocket of the blue anorak just as Paul returned. She turned it over with her hand. She felt vaguely guilty that she didn't say to him: 'Look, no harm intended but I've just taken your knife. You know, just in case.'

But she couldn't concentrate on the knife for long. The road was dangerously narrow, swerving back on itself continually, always following the contour of the river. It was beautiful and somehow oppressive at the same time. It rose up and up in the silvery sheen of the gum trees, and sometimes only the darker cypress-green of the she-oaks – like a painted shadow – told where the river lay below. The edges of the road were dangerously crumbly, even missing, and

Paul drove at little more than a standstill, with Caroline quiet beside him, until at last she couldn't help herself.

'I don't understand,' she said. 'I don't understand why you didn't warn Ellen about the brakes – that's what Jim said. That you didn't warn her that the brakes were shot. He says,' she threw a glance at her husband's profile, 'that you'd been fighting before it happened.'

Paul came to a stop.

'Yes,' he said. 'We had.' He got out. 'Come with me.'

If anybody had asked me what I was expecting to see, I couldn't have told them. I would have had no idea. I certainly would not have been prepared for such subtle evidence of disturbance: a small tree shorn in half, tyre marks, even a path, a kind of path, where the jeep had skidded and forced its way over the edge and down, down towards the river. There was no sign, of course, of the jeep itself.

I looked down and it seemed to me as if it must be only a few weeks since Ellen had died, as though – if I thought hard enough about her – I might even see the body, the wreckage, even the blue anorak that I myself was wearing at that very moment.

It made me sick to the stomach. I could smell the sweet decomposing stench of death, even though Ellen would not have stunk. She was only out there for such a short time.

I felt tears welling up and I turned away, but Paul wrenched me around again.

'Take a good long look, Caroline,' he said. 'That is where my wife died. This is where you think I killed her. Understand what you are saying when you think that of me.'

And I began to retch, dry at first, and then worse, while

all the time Paul patted me on the back, so that in the end I collapsed against him while he comforted me.

On the way back to the property, Paul told me stuff. He said he had left Ellen a note about the brakes, he had to assume she hadn't read it, that the force of the fall pushed the Landrover door open and Ellen had somersaulted through the air. The coroner had told him she would have been dead when she hit the river, but he couldn't know that for certain. 'That's the worst thing,' he said, 'the fact that she was found face down in the river. I find that the hardest thought of all to digest, that she might have drowned. It was like the ultimate irony. We bought the property because of the river, because she loves, loved, I mean, rivers, and it might have been the river that killed her.'

I imagined Ellen's body down there – I could see her so easily in a frame inside my head, a photograph not taken but somehow still existing. What is the hardest thing in the world to photograph? Death might be the obvious answer. What about the Susan Meiselaes, *Cuesta Del Plomo*? The beautiful lush vegetation with – what is that in the foreground? Look closer, a figure lying down? Something wrong with it. It is a pair of legs in jeans, a picked clean spinal cord sticking up, body parts casually strewn to one side in what looks like an advertisement for an idyllic holiday spot. Did she retch with the real stench of death in her nostrils? Or George Rodger's *Bergen-Belsen* concentration camp from 1945, the little boy strolling past piles and piles of dead bodies, so understated they could all be lying down for a nap. Perhaps the hardest thing to photograph is whatever happens to be your own personal demon. For me (for many women?) it has always been children suffering. Trite and obvious, I admit, but there is something at least about someone who has grown to adulthood – they have lived, they have stood a chance. Perhaps they have loved and fought and laughed – at least they have done that – but children? It is another matter, isn't it?

Caroline's heart (there I go again, I can't make it my heart because that would be too painful to remember) ached at the sound of his voice. At his attempt to sound natural.

'I want to show you something else,' he said.

It was the cemetery. A broken iron fence around a small, square plot of land, cleared from a patch of gum trees a few miles out of town. There were none of the signs of an English graveyard that Caroline was used to, mown grass or trimmed hedges. Here, nature was used to reclaiming her own. The dry, dusty soil scattered with rabbit holes abutted huge channels of erosion where gold miners once dug for alluvial gold. At the edge there were a few recent mounds, one of them covered in plastic flowers – what would be the point of leaving real ones out here in this climate, in this desolation? But someone had. As Caroline followed Paul through the graveyard she could see that one grave looked exactly as it should. It had been carefully tended, and there were fresh flowers in a vase, planted daisies already creeping their way to the top of the mound, and drooping fuchsias in a pot.

Paul seemed perplexed. 'What the devil?' he said, walking to that same grave. And then Caroline saw the gravestone: *In loving memory of Ellen Lucas 1938–1978*, and underneath in fine script: *Unable are the Loved to die, for Love is immortality.*

Paul looked at Caroline. 'Who did this?'

I couldn't answer. How could I? I wasn't even sure what he meant until he picked up the flowers and hurled them as far as he could.

'Who the fuck did this?'

A flock of galahs screeched in alarm and for a second I thought I could see something, a flash of something, some colour in the gum trees, but there was nothing there.

I touched him on the arm. 'Come on,' I said, 'let's get out of here.'

As if this is not enough. As if this business of Luke and writing this, and my father's sickness were not already enough, this evening when I came home, I did as I always do, had a bath, changed clothes, started to prepare the dinner. I was waiting for Karen and Harry to show up, but when the front door slammed it was just Harry who appeared in the kitchen.

'Hi love.' I was happy to see him. I have always been, will always be happy to see him. It took me a minute to detect that something was wrong, that he was filling the doorway with distress.

'I've decided to drop my film course,' he said, out of the blue, just like that.

'What?' I was still involved in the meal, the pleasant feeling of flour on my fingertips, of meat sitting waiting to be chopped, of herbs and spices. I didn't take in for a moment that there was something seriously wrong. I don't think I even heard the words, really.

'Yes,' he said, and his voiced sounded strained, almost high-pitched. 'Yes, I've decided to become a lawyer instead.'

And probably, although I can't know since I couldn't see myself, I went pale. I certainly felt as if I went pale. I went, I am reasonably sure, as white as a sheet in fact. White enough and still enough for Harry to know he had hit his mark.

'Yes,' he said. 'I've decided to become a lawyer. Like my father. Isn't that right?' He turned back towards the front door, and he said very clearly, very slowly: 'Fuck you, Mum,' and he left.

All I could think of was that Philip Larkin line, 'They fuck you up your mum and dad'. I stood there in front of the butcher's block with my still floury hands, and I knew perfectly well what had happened. My father had decided to use his illness as the ultimate weapon against my refusal to tell Harry about Paul, and as Harry had just said 'Fuck you' to me, I thought, Fuck him, that's what I thought. That was my life, my business, my choices, that's what I'd always told both of them, my mother and my father, and now here he was, my father, ruining my life again.

Quite honestly, if I hadn't had this to come and work on I don't know what I would have done. As it is I have the night ahead of me, a Harryless night I should imagine, although I am sure he is not on the streets, I'm sure he is tucked up at home with Karen, even though I have tried to ring and all I get is the answer machine.

Chapter EIGHT

So what is the relationship between the eye and the image? Simply that any image the eye – a physical structure – beholds, is, in fact the perception of an image. It is the cultural, historical and social information we bring to that image which provides us with an interpretation of the image. Discuss this in relation to the Gestalt laws of proximity, similarity, continuity and common aim. (Reference books: *The Image* by Jacques Aumont; *Organisation in Vision: Essays on Gestalt Perception* by Gaetano Kanisza; *The Optical Unconscious* by Rosalind E. Krauss.)

CS: essay subject for third-year students

So here we are and it is three days now since Harry stormed out. I have rung and left numerous messages but he doesn't ring back. I have contemplated going round there, but what for? If he's going to slam the door in my face there's no point.

I rang my father and we ended up screaming at each other. I slammed the phone down, and he's been ringing me but I'm not returning his calls. (Talk about the generation gap – my father's talking to my son, my son's not talking to me, I'm not talking to my father and if he wasn't at death's door he probably wouldn't be talking to me either.) I was right, of course, it was him, the meddling old fool. I said, straight out, 'You did it, didn't you? You just couldn't fucking help yourself. You had to interfere where you weren't wanted.' He didn't even try and deny it. Just gave me some nonsense about how he wanted to square things away in case he wasn't around for too much longer, and he'd thought about it long and hard and decided it was time for Harry to know that he did have a father, or more importantly that we knew who his father was. I screamed at him, 'It was none of your fucking business.' Next thing, his partner, my stepmother if you must, rang up and left a message on my machine. 'I don't think you should speak to your father like that. He's very upset. We're all very upset.'

They're all very upset!

I like his hide going on about fathering anyway. Who was the one who left when I was eight and spent the next eight years gadding about the world? All those postcards from Malta, the Canary Islands, Majorca, those good old expatriate places where you can get a decent beer and the locals speak English, doing his nasty little time-share holiday brochures, exhausting one market and moving on to the next. Sending letters to my mother, 'Sorry Rebecca, no money this month, a bit down on my luck. Love to Willow.' His pet name for me because he used to say my legs were as skinny as willow twigs. No sign of him for

eight years, and then la-di-dah, home again, selling insurance this time round, confident he'll make it this time round. Suddenly wants Willow to go and stay with him and his new paramour. Terrible rows when sixteen-year-old Willow says 'Get stuffed'. 'This is your doing, Rebecca,' shouting at my mother until I snatch the phone from her. 'You leave my mother out of it.' Slamming the phone down. I thought we'd made our peace over the years, but now I wonder what kind of grudge he's been carrying against me that he would go and blurt out to Harry the one thing I thought I would carry to my grave, or at least until I chose otherwise. Was that too much to ask?

These last few days while I've been wondering what to do about Harry, my writing has come to a standstill, I have been unable to write a word. Everywhere I move in the flat there are reminders of him, things I took no notice of before when he was here all the time: the Lavazza coffee he likes, Karen's green tea, his guitar, even his toothbrush. He has left so much of his life here (including his mother) – he'll have to come back, won't he?

I suppose I should be grateful that I have the exhibition to work towards. I have to keep myself occupied and this is as good a way as any. At least I have been making some progress with my photographs. I have been editing and paring back, and captioning as if my life depended on it. It is a different energy to taking photographs, or to writing. Less fractured, less obsessive. I can do it and not think about the threads of my life unravelling around me. Let's not muck around here, I'm in a terrible state about Harry. He is my life. After I came back from Australia he was my only reason for living. The sweet memories of him I carry in my heart sustain me through everything, make everything worthwhile. If he deserts me now I don't know what I will do. I just have to keep saying to myself that we will sort this out. After all, it hasn't always been sweetness and light. As a teenager he was less than keen on me for quite some time.

I stopped writing because apart from my incessant worrying, I also thought, What's the point now that he's been told – something – I don't even know exactly what, but my father's version of events at any rate. *You know your mother, she's always been difficult.* I can just imagine it. It wasn't until tonight that I realised that writing this had become essential for me. The minute I began to type this enormous sigh escaped me, seemed to come from somewhere deep within. I thought, 'At least I have this.'

But Harry and my father are not the sole cause of my worry at the moment. There's still Luke, who is now presenting me with a different kind of problem. To put it in a nutshell, over the last three days Luke has been bombarding me with notes and telephone messages. This morning he finally accosted me in the corridor, and pleaded for a second chance. He said: 'I really would just like to sit down and talk to you.' He offered to take me to dinner or lunch, whatever I wanted. In the end, I thought, What the hell? It's not like there's Harry to go home and cook for at the moment. I suggested dinner. Something mischievous stirred in me. I thought: 'Let him explain that away to his wife.'

Does it matter if I explain it from a distant point of view again, if I become The Woman again? Because that's how I feel. It's as if I am telling in the past the story of Caroline, and telling in the present this unasked for subplot which is happening externally of me. I am not sure where 'I' am at the moment. I have begun to see everything as if it's detached, apart from me. I think the only time that I am truly me is when I am at home as I am at the moment.

So they went, the man and the woman, to dinner, and to her surprise they had a good time. At least the woman had a good time. She wouldn't have presumed to say if he did or didn't, but he appeared to be enjoying himself and she'd forgotten that it could be fun to eat out with a man. She even went so far as to relax her normal no alcohol rule; she was too nervous to make it through the evening without a bit of help. At some point around the third glass of wine she forgot to be annoyed by him, forgot she'd ever been annoyed by him. Mostly they talked about photography – Lisa came up hardly at all. He simply said, 'I think I've handled it. It's okay.' And they left it at that. The woman managed, after a couple of false starts, to apologise for throwing coffee at him. She said, 'It's just you annoyed me with your assumption that I was so old and wise, you made me feel like Methuselah, if you really want to know.'

And that was when he looked at her and smiled. 'I'll tell you what,' he said, 'I was simply going crazy trying to get you to talk to me.' And then he moved on, segued easily onto something else. Would she like pudding? Coffee? Herbal tea? And what about the such and such exhibition at the Tate, had she seen it yet? – while she sat there, covered in confusion, trying to read what he had said. Then when they left, and he walked her home, he did it again. He stooped down – he was much taller than the woman – kissed her on the lips just for the briefest second, and turned around and walked away.

So that's just great. I have a pleasant dinner with someone and he makes a move. Why would an attractive married man (he wears a wedding ring, I noticed) want to have anything to do with me? And I'm not one for married men. I'm not falling into that murky soup. I think I had an idea I'd found a friend. But then there was that kiss. Short but sweet you could say. For a minute I almost wanted to ask him in then and there on the spot. I wanted to tell him everything, tell him the whole story from beginning to end, say, Listen, don't you think I was right? I know I'm right, goddamn it! I know I am. In the end I turned to this, to my story, to the screen. Anything, I reasoned, to keep me from this sensation that some enormous damage is orbiting around me just waiting to choose its moment to land.

I was far from right the night I agreed, after Paul and I had been to the graveyard, that I would stay at the farm. It was against my better judgement. It was another moment in the film where I could have stopped the action before disaster struck, and I did not.

Paul begged me to stay, and in the end I said I would, just for one night. But when he walked towards me I held my hand up. I couldn't bear for him to touch me. Especially if he didn't mean it. 'Not at the moment,' I told him. 'It's too hard.'

He nodded, but I could tell he was relieved. 'But who

was it?' he said. 'That's what I'd like to know. Someone's been visiting the grave, and it hasn't been me.'

Nevertheless. Nevertheless, Caroline blocked her door when she went to bed. She made so much noise that Paul called out: 'Are you all right?'

'I'm fine,' she shouted back, and carried on shifting furniture. No guilt attached to protecting yourself.

And when finally she fell asleep, it began, as somehow she knew it would. She could hear the sound of horses neighing, of men shouting. It was the sound of all hell broken loose, and it sent shivers down her spine. She leapt out of bed, fully dressed (a precaution: it seemed more decent than being attacked in her nightclothes). Paul's voice called out for the second time that night: 'Caroline, are you all right?'

She shouted back, 'What's that noise? It sounds like Belle.'

The handle turned. 'Can I come in?'

'Wait a minute.' Now, of course, she was in a hurry to get out and she couldn't, and all the time she could hear the sound of hooves on the wind, the sound of swearing and laughing, and somewhere behind it all, the sound, the smell of fear.

'My god.' Paul looked around at her defences in amazement. 'You must really hate me.'

'No,' she said. 'But I'm scared.'

It was a windy night that night, there a whooshing angry wind, so it was hard to tell what noise was real and what was simply my overwrought imagination, but as we stood there we both heard a burst of high-pitched whinnying. I was sure it was Belle. I knew it was Belle.

He knew too, he grabbed me by the hand and we headed outside. 'Get the torch and a halter,' he said. 'I'll get the gun.'

For a second it crossed my mind that this might be some elaborate ruse to get rid of me, but it was just for a second. It was too extreme. He was too distressed.

But by the time we got outside it was too late. The mare was gone. We stumbled around the paddock in the dark, we drove around it, we called and called, and all we could hear was the howling wind and every now and then, something else, like the sound of galloping hooves.

I asked him. 'Listen, don't you hear it?'

'It's just the wind,' he said. 'It sounds like that sometimes.'

In the end, by mutual consent, we gave up.

'We'll look again in the morning,' Paul said. 'She's probably been scared by something and got through a hole in the fence.'

But we still retired to our separate bedrooms, and mine was as busy as any Sunday race meeting. If I could have photographed it, what would you have seen? Horses galloping in the moonlight, beer cans tossed high, laughter, swearing, rough flints flying. Extreme? Maybe. At least I tried to persuade myself it was, until the minute the first rays of sun shone and I set off again. This time I hardly noticed the wallabies grazing on the dewy grass, the wild ducks on the dam, the silver sheen of frost on the gum trees. I simply plodded on, head down, looking and looking for her.

★

When Caroline found her, as she knew she would, it was even worse than she had imagined it might be. The mare was lying on her side, covered in blood. There were puncture holes in her ribs, her rump was covered in cuts, and her coat was matted with sweat. And her chest – it seemed as if someone must have ridden her repeatedly into wire, or something, it was so slashed and bloody. Even as Caroline soothed her, cradled her head in her lap, she knew there was no hope.

The vet confirmed it. 'It would be the kindest thing to put her down,' he said. 'Even if she survived, which is doubtful, it would mean months of pain. Best to put her down.'

'What do you do?' Caroline asked. 'Shoot her?'

'You can shoot her, or I'll give her an injection. It's up to you.'

'Who would do this to a horse?' Caroline's voice rose, she could hear hysteria at the edges. 'Why would anyone want to do this to a horse?'

I am rapidly coming to the conclusion that Luke is mad. The phone rang just now and I leapt to get it. Oh god, I thought it might be my Harry. I was willing it to be him. But it was Luke. He noticed.

'You sound disappointed.'

'No,' I said. 'It's just I thought you were someone else.'

I suppose, I can see that already, he must have taken it the wrong way but I wasn't about to explain my entire life to him, or why I'd rushed to pick the receiver up.

'Well,' he sounded – I don't know – hurt. 'I just rang to say I had a good night.'

'Yes. So did I.'

Then he asked me out again. And I thought, What is this? What does he want from me? I'm not young or pretty and he's married, and it's crazy, and I could feel that anger again, pure and strong, making me strong, and I said: 'Luke, it's not a good idea.'

'Why on earth not?'

'Because you're a married man, and I'm fifty-five and past my prime and used to being by myself, and the more I think about it the more I think we shouldn't see each other at all, ever. In fact I'm sure. So don't contact me, not now, not ever.' I put the phone down, and thought, Well, that's that. At least that's one complication removed from my life.

I went to make myself a cup of tea, and even before I'd got to the kettle the phone rang again. So this time I switched the answer machine on, and then I heard his voice, my boy's voice: 'Mum?' I ran from the kitchen and picked it up, but he'd gone, he'd hung up! I switched the machine off and it rang again, and I snatched it up, and it was Luke. I thought I would kill him. Before I could even speak he said: 'Look, I'm not going to hold you up, you don't have to say anything, but I'm not married.' And he put the phone down! And I sat there and thought, 'It's eleven o'clock at night and I've had more phone calls in two minutes than I usually get in two days.' I quite frankly didn't know whether to laugh or cry.

But now how can I go to bed? I'm sitting here typing this terrible thing about Belle, remembering the horror, and waiting for Harry to call again, or, okay – I'll admit it – Luke.

★

94

Caroline could hardly take on board what the vet was saying, something about a race, the midnight run.

'The midnight run?'

'Ten kilometres on a dirt road to celebrate the end of shearing. At least that's what I've heard. I've never seen it. I'd say you were unlucky – it looks like someone wanted your horse dead.'

'But why?' Her voice was high, a child's question. Why this? Why me? Why her?

Paul stood awkwardly beside her. 'Love.'

She looked at him. 'You shoot her ... it's because of you I came to this godforsaken place, now you shoot her.'

The vet was disconcerted. 'Look, I can do it. It's my job after all.'

But she was adamant. 'I want him to shoot her. He's the farmer, isn't he?' She turned to Paul. 'If you love me you'll shoot her.'

Paul shrugged. 'All right, if it's what you want.'

She bent down, kissed the mare between the ears. Closed her eyes.

'It's what I want.'

She watched while he loaded, steadied the rifle, aimed right on the forehead. Just once he looked at her, but she averted her eyes. His price to pay.

Snap. The camera in her brain took the shots. Ready.

Snap. Aim.

Snap. Fire.

Snap. A shudder, a tremor through the body, already now the carcass.

Snap. Paul put down the gun and walked away.

Snap. The vet shrugged. Packed his case, followed Paul down towards the house.

He didn't look at Caroline but the thought hung in the air: *He's got a live one there.*

One thing about the country, people still leave their keys in the ignition. At least, twenty years ago they did. I knew, as I climbed into Paul's car, exactly where I was going. This time, an authority was going to be told.

I think it was that sense of safety in the country that was most precious to me as a child, even though, of course, I was unaware of the safety, because it was simply there, all around me. Doors to houses and cars were left unlocked, the bread and meat and vegetables were all delivered, and little piles of money were left on the fridge for the travelling vans and their produce. My friends and I roamed the countryside on our ponies, swam in the river, collected eggs and helped with the milking, and that sense of safety allowed us to grow up, I think, less fearful than our city counterparts. This is not to say that we didn't have our problems; divorce or death or distress of some kind was present in all our lives, but perhaps the very proximity to nature cushioned the blows. (Ironic, then, that all those years later in Australia it was the proximity to nature which nearly killed me.)

Because I'd grown up in the country, I was determined that Harry should have the chance to experience farm life; but my mother had long since moved out of the village where I grew up, so in the end we were reduced – I felt – to the Farm Holiday. But here was the thing: Harry loved them. He was hysterical over the beauty of the baby calves, the ducklings, the hen-feeding, the inevitable cranky little pony. I never let on, not once, how much I resented spending money in order to spend time with God's creatures. (I wish he would ring ... why doesn't he ring back? And which 'he' do I mean exactly?)

My Australian experience was the first, and only, time that the country became menacing to me. I had been to some strange and dangerous places on assignment – but this was the difference: you *knew* they were dangerous, and I was not unadventurous. But this, this sense of menace I had begun to feel, was beyond my experience, and as I drove into the parks department building in Rock Forest, I was determined that someone should provide me with some kind of answer, or at least help me look for an answer to the question of Belle.

I quite like the photographs of the small bluestone building Jim worked from. I took them before I went in to tell him about Belle. There was just something about the light which demanded my attention. It didn't bother me, I had long ago got used to separating emotions from possible subject matter. When I look at them I can still see the incongruity of this small gleaming house with its neat verandah and flowerpots, set in the middle of the desolate red earth and neglect of Rock Forest. It begs the question though: What do you do about beyond the frame? This too, is something which is perhaps more fully resolved in film, the sense it can bring to you of the absolute biggest picture. It's something that Harry and I have often talked about in our late night hot chocolate pre-bed discussions. (What does he mean take up law? What an absurd idea.) It is perhaps the same discussion as time in representation, there are after all so many times functioning at once: the spectator's time, the present time, the duration of the shot, the picture, the frame, even the sense of a past or future attached to the image. I could include a picture of that shining little gem, and a viewer might conclude it was a place for Devonshire teas, or the home of someone most houseproud. They certainly would not, could not – it would be outside their frame of reference – guess that it acted as a lockup to hold drunk shearers. They would not see the deserted streets, the four-wheel drive parked outside. They might buy this picture to hang on their wall as a reminder of a quaint Australian landscape. They would not see me walking into the quiet dark inside, or Jim sitting at a high wooden bench, writing.

I pulled no punches. 'Belle's dead.'

Was it my imagination or did a flicker of annoyance cross his face? Of something more than surprise?

'How?'

I told him about what the vet had said, and the midnight run, but he was scornful, said it was an old wives' tale.

'Well,' I stuck to my guns, 'old wives' tale or not, she'd been ridden into the ground – literally.'

I think I was expecting some kind of resistance, but he showed no surprise at my desire to report the crime. (Why was I expecting resistance? After all, there was nothing to suggest that Jim was implicated in anything that had happened. I think it was simply Paul's dig about the home counties and the bullets in the sign, or perhaps I just felt out of my depth.) I told him I would be reimbursing Belle's owner, and he said he would send someone around to pick up the body. He was sympathetic, but not difficult about it. 'Bloody shame,' he said. 'She was a beaut little mare.' He told me not to worry about calling Belle's owner. 'I'll do it,' he said. 'I was the one who brought her out there. It's not your fault. Somehow I'll square it away with her. If she wants me to, I'll report it to the police. We'll find the bastards.'

Caroline nodded. Her heart felt heavy. She wanted to say, 'I could have loved her. She could have been mine.' She stood there, unsure of what to do next, not keen to drive back out to the farm, not quite yet.

It seemed Jim sensed her hesitation. 'Look,' he said, 'school holidays start tomorrow. Tourists by the busload. I've got to check a few things, make sure the mine is safe before it opens for tours. Come with me and tell me all about it. You might give me a lead. I could call the police in Bathurst if we could give them something to go on. I should call them anyway. Come with me, why don't you?'

'Yes. I'd like that.' She followed him into the bright sunshine. As they climbed into his four-wheel drive, the dainty flowers at the front of the building attracted her attention again. She looked at Jim curiously.

'Did you plant those?

'Sure. I like to garden.'

Something jogged her memory, a pattern of colour. She seemed to have seen those flowers before. But she could not bring the image forward. A shadow crossed her brain, and she wiped her forehead and sighed.

Chapter NINE

Consider that some unframed, or decentred images imply an awareness of what is happening outside the image. What is the purpose of such a technique? Is it to provoke the viewer's imagination, or to suggest that there is no life beyond the image? Please discuss, with particular reference to Henri Cartier-Bresson.

CS: from first-year photography exam, 1994; filed under E for exam, and I for image

I worked all night last night, way past the time when I realised that Harry (or Luke) was not going to ring back. By the time I'd finished I knew that the next task was to begin the alchemical process of photography. A lot of my prints are showing their age, so now, having identified my negatives I must begin my time in the darkroom. I've always loved the name 'darkroom'. As soon as I discovered that it was possible to print your own photographs I wanted to do so. My first darkroom was an old pigsty next to our cottage, where I had to crouch doubled over to work my magic. What I found, beyond the process of printing, was that devoid of all stimulus, light or noise, the darkroom could be a thing of beauty, a place of meditation and quiet. Plus, of course, the fact that no-one was allowed in. I could even pretend to be printing, and nobody would ever know. It was my world, my space.

It was in the early hours of the morning that I realised how much I was dreading this process I normally enjoy so much. I would be left alone, in the dark, bringing forth photographs from a time of terror, and the child, who unbeknown to me at the time I was then carrying inside me, would be somewhere in this city, somewhere but not with me. I would be alone with myself, alone in the dark. The thought was more than I could bear.

So it was that I decided Harry's phone call was enough of an opening to allow me to attempt communication, to transcend my own pride that had kept me, after the first few days, from contacting him.

In the car outside Karen's flat I listened to the radio, and kept an eye out for my son. It was only 7.00 a.m. I knew that sooner or later I would see his tall skinny frame, all feet and hands, and floppy blonde hair. What would I say?

I thought again of the darkroom. I'd walked in there this morning, made a list: developer, paper, pegs. I'd turned the lights off, just to try for the briefest of seconds, but it was no good: panic choked my throat.

And again, as I sat in the car, it occurred to me that dark echoed another dark.

★

When they arrived at the mine, Jim discovered he had forgotten their protective helmets.

'Damn,' he said, 'do you mind? We ought to go and get them. There's all sorts of loose stuff in there.'

Driving out to his property, Caroline realised they were on the bridle-track.

'This is the road the accident happened on,' she said.

'That's right. I was at home. I had to drive into the station and I found her on the way.'

'God. That must have been horrible.' Caroline could still see in her mind's eye that subtle disturbance – what must it have been like with a corpse in it?

'It was.' He shrugged. 'But I saw worse in Vietnam. When you've seen that much death you get used to it somehow.'

'But still, she was your friend. Wasn't she?'

'She was.'

And then we were there. At his house. Except that house is going too far, way too far, even cottage or shack would be too grand to describe the place we arrived at. The kindest thing you could say about it was that it was a soldier's domicile. Even the walls were camouflaged. If I hadn't been so surprised I might even have laughed, or teased him. And inside, neat and tidy, oh yes, but nothing – no electricity, no stove, other than a primus – nothing to indicate this was actually a home. The shower was a bucket with holes in it, the water came from a pump. It was all fine for camping, but not exactly comfortable. Not exactly normal. Although interesting to photograph, it struck me immediately.

Could Jim see what I was thinking? How odd I thought

it was? He was nonchalant. 'I don't like fuss,' he said. 'Since the war. I want to know I can move out in a minute.'

'So the enemy can't catch you?'

He grinned. 'That's right. Come on, I'll show you around.'

At first I couldn't see what he meant. There was nothing more to his lean-to that I could see, but he walked around the back of the cabin and I followed him. He reached down to pick up a large plank of wood, and as he did I saw there was some kind of trapdoor underneath. He opened it and began to climb in.

'Come on,' he said. 'It's quite safe.'

When I was having my menopause and a hot flush would strike, the sensation that would sweep over me was that I was trapped inside my own body which seemed at the time to be hell bent on betraying me. I felt it again this morning, sitting in this car, waiting for Harry. For him I knew it was still early – we're talking a lunchtime riser here – I couldn't even have begun to think about giving up. Even before I had the menopause, even as a child it was the same – the feeling of heat, beginning in my chest and spreading upwards, then downwards, a feeling so intense that I would think I must be crimson with it. Sometimes it's swept over me when I've been on assignment. I've felt if the heat communicated itself to the camera, it would become red-hot, testament to the fire in me. And even now, especially now, with the knowledge of hindsight, when I think of that underground room of Jim's, of what might have happened there, the heat begins.

★

Driving back towards the mine, the helmets on the seat between them, Caroline was silent.

'So,' he said. 'What do you think?'

She shrugged. 'Well, if anybody's going to survive World War Three, it'll be you won't it?'

'That's the general idea. Not a bad little place to bunk in for eternity.'

Caroline thought of what she'd seen, the underground home every bit as big as his cabin and more comfortable. An entire room stocked with canned food, another full of guns, knives and ammunition, a generator, a camp bed, army rations, camouflage suits. Everything, in fact, needed to sustain life . . . and something else. What? A sense of doom. Armageddon.

'I'd rather die.' She didn't realise she'd spoken out loud.

'You what?'

'I'd rather die, than live like that.'

'Not me baby, I've seen death and it ain't pretty.'

'I thought you said you get used to it.'

'You get used to it, but you don't want to do it.' He stopped the truck. 'Okay, we're here.'

A thought struck her. 'Where do you keep your poetry books?'

'What poetry books?'

Was he kidding? 'Rilke. That poem you quoted. You said you loved poetry.'

Was it her imagination? Did he pause for a moment as if stuck for an answer? But then he fell into an absurd John Wayne accent. 'I don't need no books, li'l ladyeee. I got all the poems I need right here in my head.'

Despite herself, she laughed.

★

And I thought as I sat there in the car: Why didn't I get it? Why didn't I get it? And that why was a floodgate of whys. Why didn't I tell Harry? Why won't he talk to me? Why is Luke trying to befriend – or something else – me? Why won't I ring my father when he might be dying? And the final one: *Why am I such a fucking mess at the moment?*

Even the mine looked welcoming after Jim's bunker. The entrance was an old wooden door into the hillside, which was padlocked.

He adjusted my helmet. 'It gets a bit tight once you're in,' he said. 'But stick close to me and you'll be right.'

I felt somehow macho as I switched on the torch and followed him into the dark. I didn't know – how could I know? – how quickly it would become tight; that I would have to crouch, then kneel and finally slither in order to follow him long after the pinprick of light from the entrance had died away.

I tried not to ask but couldn't help myself: 'How much further?'

'Not long. We've got a ladder coming up. It's a tight fit, but follow me up and then we're almost out.'

And it was then that I could feel the panic, the heat rising in me. As Jim began to climb ahead of me, it seemed as if he was gradually disappearing from me. I felt as if my body was expanding, that I would never be able to fit it through that tiny space. And as I began my ascent up the ladder, forcing myself up rung by rung, the nameless thing I had begun to dread flowered around me, choking and choking me. It was fear, gut-wrenching, mind-numbing fear. I had become convinced that I was going to die, like

Ellen. And as I held onto the ladder for dear life, I could feel – oh, it seemed so inevitable at the time – the rung beneath me begin to crack; and as I tried to shout upwards to Jim, there was something worse still – the light on my hat as I swung on the ladder catching a glimpse of sockets and bones, and a noise as well, and as I crashed down, I could feel this thing in the dark with me. Horrible teeth and, yes, a wide mouth – hell, perhaps on earth.

I remember I sat there on the ground shaking. I wasn't even sure I was still alive until I heard Jim's voice from above me, insistent, anxious. 'What's happened? Caroline? Caroline? Are you all right?'

I couldn't answer him, but I found I could move. I felt my legs, my ankles and feet. I seemed to be in one piece.

'Caroline . . . I'm going to get a rope. Okay?' I heard him and I nodded in the dark, as if he could see me. 'I'll pass it down the shaft, you tie it round your waist, then try climbing the ladder again. If you slip, I'll just pull you out. Okay?' I nodded again. There were tears on my cheeks.

Tears on my cheeks, a front door slamming, and a tall young man, his arm wrapped protectively around his girl-friend, walking away from me. I hadn't bargained on that. That she would be with him. I had somehow imagined that he would appear by himself, that it would be easy to get out of the car, to call his name, to mend our broken fences. But now that it came to it, I couldn't do it. Even the thought of talking to him in front of her made me feel humiliated. So I sat there in the car, watching my child stride confidently into the world, the world which for the last twenty years I had ordered and labelled and contained – the world I had made safe for him – and I felt so tired and sad and alone that I did not know where to go, what to do. So I stayed, unremarked upon, unremarkable, a fifty-five-year-old woman with grey hair, with the accompanying unkindnesses of increasing age, the lines and crinkly mouth, the thick middle-aged hands on the steering wheel, the hands which in the last few years had turned into my mother's hands.

In the sunshine at last, Caroline collapsed. 'There was a monster in there,' she said. 'It was horrible.'

Jim held her close. 'It was a bat,' he said. 'That's all. Tons of them around these mines. Just a bat. I'd never have taken you in there if I'd known that ladder was unsafe.'

'But it was in a skull!'

'It's just a sheep's skull. It's just for effect, for the kids.' And he went on stroking her hair, so that suddenly it seemed the most natural thing in the world to tilt her head up to him, to stand in the sunlight and receive his kiss on her lips. She moved her hips towards him, and he slid a hand down her spine. Every nerve in her body loosened.

But we didn't. No, I couldn't. I think it was an accumulative effect of all the stress, of Belle's death, of the terrible claustrophobia in the mine. (*Dad, I understand your fear now, I really do.*) Jim would never have been my type, it was simply reflex, and I pulled away in a minute. I remember, or do I remember? His eyes shot me this glance – or is this a memory I've made up to fit in with the rest of the jigsaw? – but he didn't push me.

'Well,' he said, 'if you change your mind you know where I am.'

But I had no intention of changing my mind. I knew enough about myself to be sure that I was not attracted to Jim, and I knew I still loved my husband. Crazy as it now seems looking back on it, I still don't think I was in any doubt that everything would work out in the end, even though another piece of the jigsaw puzzle was about to be given to me.

As Caroline got out of the truck, shielding her eyes from the sun, from the intense blue of the sky, she saw again the flowers outside the police station. Like a bolt from the blue it hit her: 'Those are the same flowers as the ones on Ellen's grave.'

He turned, how quickly he turned. 'What?'

'I said, "Those are the flowers on Ellen's grave". You planted them, didn't you? It was you who planted them.'

'So what?'

'So, isn't it a strange thing to do?'

His stillness was almost false, as if he was waiting for something to make itself clear to him before he spoke, but when he did, his tone was light.

'Why? She was my friend, and Paul could hardly do it from Sydney. It was for both of them really.'

'For both of them?'

'Sure. Why not? I was fond of her.'

'And him?'

'Of course, "and him". We were friends. I told you. Until she was killed.'

'Killed?'

'Died.'

Caroline pressed home her point. 'But you said killed, so you think she was killed, murdered . . .'

'The problem with you is your imagination works overtime. I meant, until she died.' He walked up the steps. 'Do you want me to come and get this mare, then?'

What could I do? I knew instinctively that he was not going to answer any more questions. I felt I was being dismissed.

'That would be kind.'

As I went to drive away, he called me.

'Caroline?'

'Yes?'

'I meant what I said.'

'About what?'

'If you change your mind.'

If I had changed my mind, would it have changed everything else? I don't think so.

And so I sat there in the car, sifting it over, wondering for the umpteenth time why the hell I had agreed to this exhibition, why I was putting myself through this when I could just as easily throw all those photographs out and nobody, nobody would know they had ever existed. They were never intended to exist as art, my Australian photographs, they were intended as a kind of archive for further work, for something which might have sprung into being if Paul and I had continued to go to the farm. I was gathering, that was all. Now these tiny mementoes were splintering me, and yet despite everything, I could as well their artistic possibilities. My mind was mapping the exhibition space. I could see, almost as if down a clear tunnel, where none of this other stuff, this *life* existed, a huge photograph, a tree or a rock – I wasn't sure yet – overlaid with smaller pictures. I wanted to create a chronological, almost mathematical, grid of tiny photographs, and each one would tell me: this was the farm, this was the river, this was Belle, this was the bridle-track, and on and inexorably on until the end. That would be the real way I would exorcise this story, I thought, and nobody would know. I would not have to tell anyone. And I fell asleep.

Chapter TEN

Sometimes a negative has too much contrast or is too flat to print well on any paper. If you feel the negative has potential you could try a contrast mask. A contrast mask is a weak positive or negative image on film which is registered and bound up with the original negative. The two are then printed together. A weak negative mask will increase the contrast, but if the problem is too much contrast – which is more usual – then a mask with a weak positive image should be used. The original negative is contact printed onto a sheet of continuous tone film. You can make the mask image slightly unsharp by printing it through the back of the negative, using an oblique light source and rotating the sandwiched images during exposure.

CS: notes to first-year students

'Mum. Mum.' Harry's voice was persistent, piercing the lovely layers of sleeping fog I was in.

I opened my eyes a crack, and he was there on the pavement, banging on the car window. I yawned and stretched.

'Muuuuum. Open the door.' He sounded like a child again, that extended vowel noise always indicating an unmet desire. I leant over and opened the passenger door.

'I've been trying to get you to wake up for ten minutes. I was worried, I thought something had happened.'

I was touched. 'No, I was just tired, that's all. I was up most of the night thinking about you.'

He looked suddenly shifty again, as if he was going to slip away behind the drawbridge. He shrugged. 'Well.'

'Come on Harry, love, give me a break. I've been sitting here since first thing this morning. Let's at least try and talk.'

I would like here to say what we talked about. Indeed at some point I must, in some form or other, give you that image. The mother and son in a greasy café, him with a coffee, her with a tea. The intensity of the conversation, the questions and answers, the occasional wiping of tears on both sides. I would like to. But something else so extraordinary happened to me this evening that I must write it down first. I am bursting with it, full with it. At this moment Luke is asleep in my bed.

There.

As defined by Barthes there are two kinds of photographs – the photographer's photo and the spectator's photo. The first kind is objective, it activates information, it contains codes; the second is subjective and in it the photograph represents a part-object of desire, uncoded, chanced upon. The photographer's photo must be decoded by the spectator, the spectator's photograph must spawn a subjective relationship between the viewer and the photograph. This whole theory, of course, is somewhat dubious because it relies on Barthes' own subjective experience, and it also begs the question: can you create a photographer's photo from a spectator's subjectivity?

For instance: I stand in the doorway of my room, and for the first time in several years a man is asleep in my bed, and there is something about *how* he is lying there, his limbs thrown every which way, the sheet up to his waist, his whole body spreadeagled across the bed, which both delights and terrifies me. But the light – it's a full moon and the light is pouring in through the window – and everything is there to create a technically masterful photograph, with the final irony that the photograph would be of a photographer, but I can't quite bring myself to take it for so many complex reasons. If this never happens again, I don't want to have a physical memory of it, I don't want to take him while he is unaware of it and I am scared that it is so long since I have taken a photo loaded with imagery that I won't be able to do it. That the result will be less than the reality. And what's the point of that?

Today was one of those days when the whole day itself had an air of unreality about it, starting with my vigil outside Harry's flat, and ending, well, here with the moon and the sleeping figure, the man who has just become my lover.

And he became my lover because I got angry with him again, and tried to throw him out, but he wouldn't have it, and that terrifies me too. The implications are all too enormous.

The chronology, the archival material is simple enough. Harry and I talked for some time (I will come back to this, flesh it out, but for now, this will have to do). He went to college, I went to work, late. I bumped into Luke as I was heading out of the college. I was desperate to get home, to have a bath, change clothes, think about what had happened with Harry. But we bumped into each other. And one thing led to another. Oh god. That doesn't really work, does it? One thing led to another. Of course it did, and of course it didn't. And yet, doesn't one thing always lead to another?

If, for instance − and I know I am skirting around the edges here, but I will have to bring myself through all of this slowly and with care − but if, for instance, I had not gone to report what had happened to Belle to Jim, if I had telephoned him instead, would Paul have then made a bonfire, which when I arrived back at the farm (not home, never home any more) was burning near the woodpile, dangerously near the woodpile? If one thing leads to another, was it my absence which led to that?

I could see the smoke from the top of the rise above the farmhouse. I didn't think too much of it; as a country child bonfires were a constant. It wasn't until I got out of the car and moved closer to Paul that I noticed that this was no ordinary rubbish, no indeed. There was a chair in there, and material, items of clothing, and I thought, as I turned to look at him, and saw his face streaked with dirt and dust and ash, I thought, he is mad, he is actually mad. And as I thought it, I began to focus on what was in the fire – I could see a chair leg, some curling photographs, a shirt sleeve. Paul was holding a dark green scarf in his hand, and it dawned on me that it was mine.

Caroline was shocked. 'That's my scarf!'

'No. It's Ellen's.'

'My God, Paul, there's a ton of my stuff in there.' She scrabbled around the edges of the flames but she was too late.

He seemed unconcerned, detached. 'It's all Ellen's,' he said again. He didn't seem to notice the sound of a truck, and doors banging up by the gate. Caroline could hear Jim's voice shouting something out. So she waited, watching Paul as he stoked and prodded.

When Jim arrived he looked at her curiously. 'What's going on?'

She chose her words carefully: 'Paul's burning stuff.'

'Yeah, well, it's not real sensible just at the moment, mate.' He spoke to Paul's back. 'It could get away on you.' He turned to Caroline. 'Are you okay? We've come to get the mare.'

She pointed up towards the dam. 'She's over there.' Then tried to drop it in casually. 'I might come back into town with you.'

For a second Paul stopped what he was doing. 'No,' he said. 'I need you here.'

'Sure.' Jim smiled at her. 'We won't be long and we'll come back for you.'

'Didn't you hear me? I said "no".'

'Come off it, Paul. You're a big boy. Your wife wants out.'

Paul turned to face his adversary, his face blackened and smudged, his eyes red-rimmed and watering. 'This is none of your business.'

'Oh, but I think it is, mate . . . I reckon your wife can leave when she bloody well likes. You look like shit, by the way.'

You know, looking at it in retrospect all these years later, it was almost funny really. So surreal and bizarre – the dead horse, the madman and the fire, the blockish oafs Jim had brought with him, and Jim standing there, tall, bearded, like a bushranger, absolutely sure he was going to get his way. Perhaps it was that sense of arrogance in Jim that prompted Paul to do what he did next. What can he possibly have been thinking? Perhaps in his madness he thought it would be an even match. But as he launched himself at Jim, Jim simply began to land punches, almost as if he was squashing a fly. It was more than I could bear. It was one thing knowing Paul was mad, it was another seeing him destroyed in front of me.

'Leave him alone!' Caroline screamed. She threw herself on Jim's back, clawing at him, but he flicked her off.

'Help me!' she shouted at Jim's offsiders, but they stayed where they were, still as stone.

'For fuck's sake . . .' She screamed again, and at last they moved. It took the two of them to pull Jim off the crumpled body on the ground.

'Get out.'

She leant over Paul to check his pulse, and got a tissue from her pocket to wipe the blood from his chin and his lips.

'Caroline.' Jim reached out a hand towards her.

'Just take the mare and get out.'

'But what about you? I thought you wanted to come.'

'I'm hardly going to leave him like this, am I? What came over you?'

'I don't know. It's just, well, he can't tell you what to do. You can leave. You wanted to leave.'

'I can still leave. I don't need your help . . .' She stood up.

'He doesn't know how lucky he is.'

'Well. He's lucky to be alive at the moment. Now get the mare and go.'

'If that's what you want.'

'It is.'

And what of Paul? What did he think while he was lying there on the ground? Shall I hazard a guess?

Paul watched them from the ground. He could hear. Could hear him trying to honey her. He wanted to spit, but his tongue was swollen, there were ants and dirt and ash in the corner of his mouth. He saw the men's boots disappearing from sight, the feel of Caroline's cool hand on his head. He groaned. (*That couldn't be too far from the truth, and he certainly did groan.*)

★

Inside in the dark, she bustled about, she sat him on a chair in the kitchen and got a bowl of warm water with disinfectant.

'Ow.' He winced. 'That hurts.'

'You're lucky it's not worse.' She kept up her dabbing. 'I thought he was going to kill you.'

'Would you have been sorry?'

'Of course.'

'But you were going to leave with him.'

'Not *with* him,' she said, surprised. 'Not with him. I was just going to get a lift to Bathurst – to catch a plane back to Sydney.'

Paul groaned. 'Jesus, my head.'

'Here.' She poured them both a whisky. 'This should help.'

So perhaps, dear reader, or if that is you Harry, my darling Harry, perhaps you begin to see – as I too only just begin to see as I write this – why I have not been so very good with men. And we are not yet at the kernel, not at the worst bit. There is still a little way to travel to the worst bit, the nucleus without which there would be no story. I think that when I write that bit many things will fall into place, for you and for me, and perhaps you will be more forgiving of the decisions I made, because, despite our talk this morning I could not quite bring myself to tell you the worst bit, to give you my confession. I have always known that it is not from my child that I must find absolution.

Chapter ELEVEN

One day, all of you may look back on one particular moment in your lives when you decided to become a photographer. Mine, curiously enough, came to me in a dream. One night I dreamt I was on a street in Paris, outside a hotel. There was a woman getting out of a taxi, and porters were collecting her bags for her. I asked someone next to me who she was. 'Oh that's Margaret Bourke White,' the man said. 'She always stays at that hotel.' In the dream he looked at me closely. 'You're a photographer too, aren't you?' 'Yes,' I said. 'Yes, I am.'

CS: filed under talks, speeches and essays, 1990

Which brings me back, one thing leading to another, to Luke. (I could write this sentence a hundred times over and still be in the same place. I am not yet ready to talk of us in the first person, if I ever will be ready – which I doubt, despite his sudden arrival in my life.)

So I tell you in the only way I can: the man wanted to buy the woman a drink after work.

Why did I agree? A combination of tiredness, the stress of the day, knowing there was nothing there for me at the flat, only this story and my photographs, the darkroom demanding my attention. And, yes, of course, a sense of desire to know what he meant by saying, 'I'm not married'. And yes, there was the kiss. So I weakened and said yes.

There, I almost managed it for a minute.

So we sat in the pub with our drinks, and it was companionable in almost the same slightly odd way that it was companionable sitting in the farmhouse kitchen with darkness falling outside, with Paul nursing his sore head, and both of us nursing our whiskies.

I have a choice now, don't I? I can go back or forwards again. But back is still where the pull is. I think I cannot truly move forward until I have sorted out back.

So back I will go again.

I asked Paul, I remember, trying to keep it light, conversational. 'Why did you burn all that stuff anyway?'

His face contorted, sitting there in the dim light. He put his head in his hands. 'I just wanted to get rid of her. I keep seeing her, hearing her.'

'Did it work?'

'I don't know.'

'But why would she haunt you?'

'I don't know.'

And again, wham, a piece of the jigsaw puzzle fell into

place. 'It's because of me,' I said. 'Isn't it? It's because of me.'

'No.' But the look on his face said it all. He didn't need to tell me anything else. I didn't know what to say. How do you fight a dead woman? I got up to put the kettle on. I was thinking about my next move, how to approach the fact that something had to give, that one of us − me − or both of us, had to get out of there. And then suddenly he spoke again.

'She was pregnant, you know, when she died,' he said, conversationally. 'She was pregnant, only just. Seven or eight weeks, she thought. She didn't want it, she told me that morning. We'd been trying for a baby for years, and when she found she was pregnant, she told me she didn't want it.'

When I turned around, he was crying.

'This is the one thing I cannot explain to myself, why she didn't want to have my child.'

Is Paul's story − or his story of his life with Ellen − on my mind because of Luke's story? After all they were not dissimilar. Long-term marriages both of them, no children in Paul's story, three in Luke's. But it is not quite fair, despite the apparently limited number of plots involved in human lives, to blend them together. One person's broken marriage is not, after all, another person's broken marriage.

But it is still, at this stage, Paul I know best, isn't it? Or the Paul of twenty years ago anyway. And the purpose, if this fulfils its purpose, is for Harry to know why I never told him about his father. So to honour some sense of obligation − and yes, I'll admit it, to continue my act of cowardice, the difficulty of describing the journey from the pub, to home, to a row, to bed – I should speak of Paul and Ellen first. And it takes me closer to the heart of the matter. Much closer to the heart of the matter.

Perhaps now that I am getting used to this writing down, perhaps I can take a liberty and tell this story from Paul's point of view. He did have a point of view. I will concede that, and I knew him, after all, well enough by then to hazard a guess or two.

Paul told her they had started fighting a year or two before Ellen's death, about little things: him spending too long at work; her insistence on a heavy social life; how they'd always planned to have children one day, but when he started pushing the idea, she seemed to withdraw from it. He thought – he felt treacherous even voicing the words – that she might be having an affair. It's just, he said, she grew so distant ... I never thought it would happen to us.

He fell silent. He wished he could conjure Ellen up in front of him. What would he say to her? *You told me you were pregnant, and I leapt up and went towards you, my arms outstretched, and you turned away from me and said, 'But I don't want it'. And I was stunned. I swear I felt the chill of death on the house at that moment, on my unborn child, even on you.*

Caroline's voice pierced his reverie. 'So what happened?'

'We had a fight. We went to bed in separate bedrooms.' He could feel his chest becoming constricted with the effort of explanation. 'In the morning I woke up early ...' He could hear his voice, disembodied, detached, as if he was telling the story as he had had to at the time to the police, to the coroner, to Ellen's family. 'I took the Landrover to go and get some wood, and that's when I discovered the brakes were dodgy. They were working but not well, you had to pump them to get any connection. When I got home I decided I had to get out of there for a while, so I left a note warning her not to drive the Landrover and I went into Bathurst in the car to do some shopping – tools and general farm stuff. When I got back she was gone. I was upset, but not too worried. I thought she'd just gone into town, read my note and decided to go in slowly – after all in a four-wheel drive you can use the gears as brakes if you need to, and she was a good driver. I had no idea she'd drive the bridle-track. I still have no idea why she was there. Then I got a call from Jim saying he'd found her.'

'God.' Caroline's face was as white as a sheet. He felt sorry for her; he'd tried to protect her from it. Tried to protect himself from having to tell it again. Yet somehow there was a kind of relief in it. He had no idea how tightly he'd been holding on, and now, at least, there was some sense of release. 'People say I murdered her, perhaps I did. Perhaps I did. For a long time after I couldn't feel anything, go anywhere, and then you came along and life seemed as if it might have some purpose again . . .' His voice trailed off. 'I'm sorry, Caroline. I really am.'

'Why do you think she didn't want it?'

The question took him by surprise. 'What?'

'The baby. Why do you think she didn't want the baby? She must have had a reason.'

He thought about it. 'She had reasons,' he said. 'But none of them made much sense to me. How could they?'

'But what did she say?' Caroline was persistent. He

shrugged. He couldn't see why it was important, himself. He could still see his wife, his dead wife, that is, standing in front of him. He wasn't up to passing on that conversation, that strange conversation.

What did you say? You said it wasn't the right time. That you'd been a career woman too long, that you'd been meaning to talk to me about a vasectomy, and now this had happened and you'd realised that after all you didn't want to have children, and do you know what? I didn't believe a single word of it and I still don't.

'She said it wasn't the right time.'

'Is that all?'

'You sound like the inquisition.'

'But you've got to admit that it seems strange. After everything that's happened, I'm entitled to ask.'

'Yes.' He nodded. 'I can't tell you any more, Caro. She told me she was a career woman, that was about the end of it. I don't know, I'd always thought we'd do both.' He stretched and yawned. 'I don't know about you, but I'm bushed. I'll make a cup of tea.'

That was it. Sort of. It seemed as if, at least for him, the air had been cleared. How I wished that he had told me all this before. How I wished I'd asked more questions before. I've always been nosy, and yet there I was, married to someone whose wife had died and I'd scarcely asked a question – for fear of what? Seeming rude? Stiff upper lip and all that. And I can read what I've written and see that Paul still did not really understand what I was getting at. That the thing I wanted to do more than anything else in the world was to ask Ellen why she did not want to bear her husband's child. It seemed to me as if this was the answer to the riddle, the missing part of the jigsaw. It didn't seem to occur to him that Ellen might not have been telling the truth. It was as if, as a woman, I sensed that this was where the truth lay, and that there was something dark and female about it, a lie by omission perhaps. And again, how I wish that the fog had lifted then. To look back with clarity upon confusion is most upsetting. It is hard, no, it is still impossible, to forgive myself for not working it out earlier, or then, or even just a tiny bit later, a tiny bit before it became too late. Only the tiniest bit to go to that moment from which there is, was, never was, any chance to draw back. Fate? Karma? Or just plain bad luck? Or for what I could also not forgive myself, lack of judgement.

But also, Paul was right: I was, as he put it, bushed.

A wave of tiredness swept over her. She would have liked to have said to him, 'But she was lying. Or you are lying. This is not the whole story.'

'I've got to rest,' she said. 'While you were busy practising pyromania, I was stuck in a mineshaft with Jim.' (Already several melodramatic adventures before. Was I a glutton for punishment or what? I had learnt, as a photographer, to put up with uncomfortable circumstances. I was used to hardship and, of course, few if any boundaries around danger. I blame my parents for that. Why not? One of them's dead, the other one probably dying. And there has been more movement on that front too, but how many subplots can one person carry?)

'Jim again.'

'I went to report Belle to him. He suggested I might like to look at some local history. One of the ladder rungs broke. I got stuck. End of story.'

'You poor thing.' He stood up and moved towards her but this time it was she who flinched away. 'I'm sorry,' he said again, both of them knowing that the word was hopelessly inadequate.

'Anyway,' she said, 'why do you hate him so much? What's he ever done?'

'I don't know. Nothing.'

Yet would he, perhaps, if the circumstances had been different, been able to confess what I suspect was the truth – that Jim made him feel small, and that also he could not forgive him for finding Ellen? Maybe he even thought, in his unhealed mind, that if Jim had not found Ellen she would still be alive. There is after all no logic connected to grief. But I think he, as a city dweller, envied Jim's ease with the bush. I don't suppose that it ever occurred to him how badly Jim would have dealt with his environment, and that not every woman wants a cowboy, at least not forever. Even in my short time in Australia it seemed to me there was a far greater divide between city and country than there is in Europe, and why not? The cities are so far away, the bush so remote. Even the idea of a weekender a good five hours' drive away from London or New York or Paris would be absurd. For holidays perhaps, but not for weekends. But there we were, in the kitchen of our weekender, a five-hour drive from Sydney, a good country hour from the nearest town, and we might as well have been on another planet.

★

'So,' said Caroline. 'What now?'

'I don't know about you, but I'm tuckered out.' He headed towards the bedroom, towards their bedroom. 'Shall we lie down together?'

'I don't know.'

'Well, let's try,' he said. 'Let's at least lie down and sleep.'

So that is what they did. They lay down next to each other almost cautiously, as if a line had been drawn down the middle of the bed, until Paul reached out for her hand and held it, and gradually she allowed her stiffly jointed fingers to relax, so that in the end they slept together as the night fell, and the moon rose and set.

As the first glimmering rays of dawn were touching the tips of the gum leaves Paul turned to her and whispered, 'Ellen, Ellen. You've come back.' So quietly he said the words that for a moment she could not be sure what it was he had said, until they came again, slipping his betrayal through his still sleeping lips. 'Ellen. I love you.'

And with that Caroline knew finally what she must do. She oh so silently slipped from the bed, carrying her clothes with her, and in a minute, in the time it took her to do her teeth, to splash her face, relieve herself, she was gone, out of there. As she left she picked up the anorak – it seemed symbolic somehow to her that she should take the last of Ellen's things from the house.

She walked through the crisp cool beginning of day towards the road, towards freedom.

Chapter TWELVE

The optical arts spring from the eye and solely
from the eye.

Jules Laforgue, 'Impressionism'

It makes it sound romantic, doesn't it? In a way, I mean, sad but romantic, the lonely woman trudging off, leaving her husband with his ghost. I wonder what would have happened if that *had* been the end of the story?

I suppose if Luke was to read this perhaps he would think that even then I was being a coward, not seeing something through to its natural conclusion. And of course if I had stayed with Paul, life might have been very different. (But Luke does not know what comes later, just around the corner, about to catch up with me on that road while I walk along waiting for a farmer and a lift to Bathurst. In my mind: Bathurst/London. Not even a stop-off at the flat to pick up my things. No way. I will get Paul to ship them to me, and after all I have always travelled light. I will buy anything I need at the airport. I have my passport, I have my camera, I have some money and my credit cards. I am in the habit of carrying my passport everywhere in case of a sudden assignment. Lucky for me, I think. I will be on a plane to England, to safety, in no time and this will all become like a bad dream. I will recover from it. I did not know, as Luke does not know twenty years later, that the bad dream is about to become a nightmare.)

This is what Luke called me – a coward – earlier when we were fighting. And in fairness to these two parallel stories, although I did not foresee this one – how could I? – I must now backtrack just a little. I must leave me walking along the side of the road, and explain just how and why Luke has come to be in my bed.

Even this, actually, if you must know, is an act of cowardice although it hurts to admit it because of the heart of the matter to which we are coming, because now that I have arrived at my destination I have no desire to write it down. In a way I now understand Paul's reluctance to talk about Ellen's death. I do not want to tell this part of the story. It has been locked up for too many years. But it must be said, or it would leave a gaping hole. This would not then explain to you, Harry, why I behaved as I did.

Which is what Luke and I had the row about.

We chatted our way back to my flat. I think we were putting off any meaningful communication until we got back there. I think we both knew the pub or the street corner or the taxi was no place to explain ourselves to each other. So I invited him back, to talk, or so I thought. I think I really thought that.

And at some point during our conversation he asked,

explaining his divorce, Had I not noticed that his wedding ring was on his right hand, not his left hand? And I told him casually, 'Oh, by the way, when I said I was expecting someone else on the phone it was my son Harry I was talking about, not another man.' While we were readying ourselves to get these signals clear – we were both available and interested – I made a tactical error. I told him about the row with Harry and why he was not speaking to me and why I'm not speaking to my father. (Well, actually I am now, but the communication is somewhat abbreviated. I am still mightily pissed off.) I didn't tell him *this* story, the story of Caroline and Paul and the Heart of the Matter. Why should I? I have no idea yet whether I can fully trust him. But I told him that I had good reasons for not telling Harry who his father was, and anyway, that it was up to me to tell him, not my father.

And Luke sat there, very quietly on my couch, his fingertips touching, a frown on his face, and at some point as I paused in my rant against ungrateful teenagers, he said: 'You know, as a father, I think you're wrong. Correction: as a father, I *know* you're wrong. You might have done it for all the right reasons but you've denied Harry and his father the chance to ever really know each other. Even if they meet now, you've denied both of them twenty years of their lives.'

I looked at him in astonishment. 'I thought you'd understand.'

He was distressed. 'How could I understand that, Caroline? I'm a father myself. It's one thing to choose not to acknowledge a child, or to have nothing to do with it, it's another to be denied the knowledge that you have one, or for a son to be told he has no father when he does. Can't you see that?'

'No.' I stood up. 'I can't and quite frankly I don't think it's any of your business. In fact I think it would be a very good thing if you left.'

And there it was again, that anger, clutching me in the stomach, the chest, the throat. That fucking bastard, daring to make a judgement on *my* life. Had I made one on his? Christ, he used to be a fashion photographer. A fashion photographer! What kind of useless profession is that? (Actually I don't really mean that. In many ways I think the great fashion photographers are social historians – they capture life for us in a way that nothing else, not even a painting, can.) But at that minute I wanted him out – out of my flat, out of my sight.

The only problem was, he wouldn't go.

'You can't go about running away from people all your life,' he said. 'Throwing them out, or throwing things at them, or cutting the cord every time they disagree with you.'

I'm not proud of myself, I have to admit, but I yelled at him, 'I'll bloody well do what I like.'

'Of course you will,' he said. 'I'm not trying to stop you, I'm only putting a different point of view.'

I felt all disturbed, all shook up as the song says. I suddenly got a flash of that dream, the man who wouldn't argue, and worse, these images: my father storming out of the house, my mother weeping, 'Oliver please don't go,' and me clinging to her skirts. Like a kaleidoscope they tumbled out: the rows, the slamming of doors, the hanging up on the phone. 'Willow, Willow, I love you.' Me putting the phone down, me storming out. And later, me threatening my mother with my imminent and permanent departure. And I stood there, while Luke waited.

'Go.' I said it again, and I meant it. 'Please go.'

And again no argument. 'All right, if it's what you want.'

'It's what I want.'

And I stood there, waiting for him to leave. Wanting him to be gone with every fibre of my being, so I could cry, so Willow could cry, and he was almost gone, but then he turned and walked towards me and held his arms out and somehow I found myself in them.

And all I am going to say here is, as I said before, that one thing led to another and that is enough for anyone to know. But before we fell asleep we talked way into the night, and I began to tell him this story, I began to try and explain why I was right not to tell Harry about his father, but it was too complex, and despite the row and despite the sex, he simply said, before he dozed off, 'There can't have been a reason good enough.'

Which is what woke me.

Was the reason good enough? For the first time ever I doubt myself. Have I denied my child something so precious that he will never be able to forgive me? I cannot answer that question. I cannot ask for a judgement until the final bit of the story is told. Perhaps once it is written I will be able to explain to them all, perhaps the secret will not become so terrible and my reasons will become clearer.

So let us return then to the woman on the side of the

road. And let us say that at last she heard a vehicle. She thought it might be Paul, but when she turned around to put her thumb up, she was somehow unsurprised when it turned out to be Jim.

'You must have second sight,' Caroline said, hauling herself up beside him.

'If I had second sight you wouldn't have already walked this far,' he said, looking at her curiously. 'What are you doing up at this time of day?'

'I've run away,' she said.

'Lucky for you I came along, then. I'll take you to Bathurst. I've got an early appointment with the boss – someone's laid a complaint against me.'

'Really? Who?'

'I don't know. I thought it might be you.'

'Why on earth would it be me?'

'Because I hit Paul.'

'Ah. Well, I was upset but I'm not a telltale.'

'I thought you might be.'

'Well, I'm not.'

'Good-oh.' He whistled a few bars of 'Yankee Doodle Dandy'. 'That's all right then.'

It was so strange driving back along that road at Jim's breakneck speed, so different to my optimistic arrival there only a few days before. I looked out of the window at the trees along the fence line, heavy with dust from the dirt road. I would miss them, I thought, that drab olive green I found so beautiful. I would miss the physical landscape if nothing else, and as if he read my mind, Jim said: 'So, will you miss me?'

'What?' Caroline had been staring out of the window.

'Will you miss me?'

'Jim, I don't know.'

'We'd have made a good couple, you and me.'

'Maybe.' Not the time she thought to reject him out-right. What was the point? She'd be out of here in no time. When he put his hand on her leg, she lifted it off gently enough and he merely smiled.

'You can't blame me for trying.'

'No.'

'I thought,' he said, 'I thought perhaps you might be like Ellen. I thought it might be something to do with English girls. That perhaps you liked to fuck blokes from the bush. No harm in a bit of rough trade.' He whistled unconcernedly. Did not even look across at her.

Caroline experienced a sudden and curious sensation of déjà vu, as if she had been operating with a cloudy film over her eyes, as if all along someone had been trying to tell her something and only now, too late, was it becoming clear.

'What do you mean?' She could hear her own voice, high and strained, as if something – what? – was riding on the answer.

'Oh, come on,' he said. 'Don't play the innocent with me.'

'I don't know what you're talking about.'

'As if Paul wouldn't have told you.'

'Told me what?' She felt as if she was stuck in a maze.

'About me and Ellen.'

'You and Ellen?'

'You sound like a parrot. Me and Ellen. About Us. About Our Affair.'

Snap. Change the depth of field. Bring the foreground close. Focus. Stay still.

'You had an affair with Ellen?'

'Two years, on and off. Whenever they came up, really. I never was much of a one for the city . . . So Paul's never mentioned us, then.'

Slowly. To photograph wild animals, you have to stay crouched and camouflaged for the longest time. Don't scare the horses. Don't scare yourself. Don't say the wrong thing.

'Perhaps he didn't know.'

'Of course he fucking knew. That's why she stopped it. Came to see me and told me it was all over. Biggest mistake she ever made. Said it was because he knew.'

My mind. My mind raced: *Jesus, Paul, was that the secret? Was that what you wouldn't tell me? Why didn't you tell me?*

'So that was why she was at your place.'

'That's right.'
'But you were the one who found her.'
'That's right.'

The shutter, in the dim light, opens and closes slowly, allowing as much available light in as possible. As the light increases, so does the shutter speed. And as she thought, so her brain raced faster and faster, and just at the moment of clarity, just as she was about to open the door and jump, he stopped the truck, and before she could say or do anything, she was slammed up against the passenger door, his hand on her throat.

'What a shame,' he said, stroking her hair with his free hand, for all the world like a lover.

She gasped for breath. 'Let me go.'

He laughed. 'God, no.'

She screamed. 'I don't care if you killed her, just let me go.'

'Shhh. You'll wake the neighbours.'

Still he pinned her to the door, almost as if she was a butterfly. He pulled out a cigarette and lit it, using his elbow in her throat, instead of his hand, until he had it lit and in his mouth.

'When I saw her,' he said, for all the world as if he was telling her a story to pass the time, 'come bumping down the track in the beat-up old Landrover, I was so pleased to see her. What a fool, eh? I had no idea she was going to dump me. She was in a state, said the brakes weren't gripping. She was shaking. I told her not to worry, I'd fix them up, and she came inside. I put my arms around her, to hold her, and she pushed me off. Pushed me off!'

I sat there and I listened. I was transfixed. I wanted to get away, desperately I wanted to get away. Every nerve ending was tingling while I watched and waited, but there was no chance, not then, not while he was telling this story. But there was this – while he was speaking, I was alive and while I was alive, I had a chance.

'I should have seen what was coming, I suppose, but I didn't,' he went on. 'She told me Paul had found out, that he was in a terrible state, that it was over. Well, I beat the place up a bit. I was distraught.' He looked at Caroline. 'I loved her. That's the hard part. I really did love her, but she wouldn't be moved. She preferred that poncy little prick to me. Even now that rankles. "I've got to go," she said. "He's waiting for me. He doesn't know I'm here." I said, "You can't go with the brakes like that." I was trying hard to be oh so polite, oh so grown-up about it. But when I saw the truck, that's when I realised. So easy, my god, she'd signed her own fucking death warrant. Instead of fixing the cable, I cut it. I knew she wouldn't use the brakes until she was at the top of the hill, no need. She knew the road like the back of her hand anyway, and I told her: "Don't use them until you have to because they're dodgy." I made sure, you see, she wouldn't use them until she really needed them, in case she worked out they were shot. I didn't wave her goodbye. She looked at me with this puzzled expression and for a minute I thought she might be about to say something else, but then she turned the key, and that was it. She was off.'

For a brief second Caroline closed her eyes, tried to block him out, imagine him out of the truck, erase him into thin air. Even that slightest movement was enough to cause him to turn towards her.

'Offended your English sensibilities, have I?' he said. 'Ellen was like that too. She often thought I was coarse, but it was what she liked as well. The first thing she did when she saw me was to smell my sweat. Said it turned her on.'

God, was that true? To think that Ellen could be unfaithful to Paul with him. I have never thought about her before in this picture. What did she bring to her marriage, what was her story? It's like that photograph by Laszlo Moholy-Nagy, *Jealousy*. The shadow man standing in the frame, and a woman in a bathing suit stepping out of the frame, and then diagonally behind them is another shadow couple, and inside one of them is this tiny, tiny image of this woman, and she's holding a line which goes directly to the bathing suit woman's heart, and you think, when you look at it: Who are these women? Is one of them having an affair with the other one's husband? Is one of them simply jealous of the other? In a sense Ellen above all was the one holding the line, wasn't she? I was simply a continuation of the plot. Certainly that's how Jim seemed to see me, even at that point when he was telling me his gruesome tale.

Chapter THIRTEEN

No-one can advise anyone else what to do in the face of danger, but pose yourselves this question: In a dangerous situation would you continue to take photographs?

CS: lecture notes

A question Harry might put to me: Why were you attracted to my father in the first place? A question I might put to myself as well, of course. He was unlike any other man I'd been attracted to – at least he seemed to be. He seemed, when I met him, to be an easygoing man, someone who was uncomplicated, someone to whom life was simple. Someone quite unlike me. I think if I had met him in England I wouldn't even have looked at him, he would have seemed too nice, too ... available for me. I suppose in a way Sydney was like a shipboard romance for me. It was so beautiful, the climate so perfect, one almost had to fall in love. I have wondered about Paul over the years, whether Ellen was the only reason for his increasing neurosis, whether he recovered enough to remarry. In the few months we had together in Sydney he always seemed sane. A little sad sometimes. He had an expressive mouth, it could down-turn at the edges quite easily, and I knew at those times just to let him be. If he had not insisted on returning to the farm for our honeymoon – if he had simply sold it and moved on – our lives might have been very different. Although I suppose the past always catches up with you somehow, which is what I have been finding out in spades over the last few weeks. But we did have an idyllic few months. At least we had that. I suppose I could narrow the focus even further and say that it was not the farm or Paul or even Ellen that did us in. It was Jim.

To save her life, and she was pretty sure this is what it was coming down to, Caroline sat very still. She tried to remember all the things she'd learnt on assignments in difficult places, how to placate aggressors. She could recall a veteran of war zones telling her to stay still and if she got a chance, to talk. 'It's hard,' he said, 'even for a mad bastard to shoot you if you're talking to them.' But at this moment the mad bastard next to her wasn't letting up. Not for a second.

'I made sure,' he said, 'that I left nothing to chance. When she drove out just for a minute I regretted what I'd done. I thought perhaps if I ran, I'd have time to head her off, to warn her at the top of the hill. I could take a shortcut from my place cross country and straight up, and get to the corner before her. Ran like the wind, I did, through the scrub, through the trees, sounded like a herd of fucking elephants, the sound of the gum leaves crunching under my boots. I got there before her all right, but somehow though, when I got there, I changed my mind. I climbed up the bank and watched her. Nothing like the satisfaction of a job well done. That's what I liked about 'Nam. When you laid a trap and blew the fuckers sky-high. It was perfect. She never even knew I was there. She came around the bend, put the brakes on and sailed straight off the corner.'

I remember: he seemed to smile. I remember how much I wanted to wipe that smirk off his face, how much I wanted to get away. He turned to me, said casually: 'You've gone white. People do that when they're in shock.' Another little pleasure for him, no doubt.

Something else occurred to Caroline. 'Belle too?' she said. 'Did you kill Belle?'

'Jesus, no. What do you think I am?'

Now that was an interesting question at that point in time, wasn't it? I refrained from answering.

'Well who did?' Caroline said, desperately aware she was playing for time. Would he notice? Would he slip up?

'Anybody could have.' He shrugged. 'They all hated Paul, you know, even before Ellen died. The locals hate all the Pitt Street farmers, with their fucking four-wheel drives and their fifty-dollar bills. They fucking loathe them ... even more than they loathed me when I first

141

came here, but I knew how to win them over. Not like Paul, he never worked it out. He always thought it was to do with spending money, stupid fucker. He never even realised how much that pissed them off. He'd pay them to do his fencing, and they'd steal his sheep. He'd report it to me and he and I would pretend I was going to do something about it. I know what you're trying to do by the way, and it won't work . . . Still, anything else while you're at it?'

'The poetry . . . it was Ellen who taught it to you, wasn't it?'

Jim grinned. 'You're sharp, aren't you? Here you are all bailed up and you're still looking for answers. But no, you're wrong on that one, we both loved poetry. It was something we had in common. I wonder what *we* might have shared? I guess we'll never know now because it looks as if Paul is going to lose another wife in an accident. Careless of him. In fact downright criminal, I'd say.' He brought himself up close to her face, so close she could feel his breath. 'But first we're going to have some fun, pussycat. I'm going to give you a fighting chance.'

Her eyes closed for the briefest of seconds. He wasn't going to kill her. He grabbed his gun. 'I'll give you twenty seconds and then wham-bam, I'm after you. Go on.' He opened the door, so that with the sudden release of pressure, she tumbled out. 'Piss off.'

She needed no second bidding. She was off and running, her sides already heaving. Sobbing, 'Oh god, oh god.' Straight down towards the valley below. Stumbling on rocks. Didn't dare look behind her. Instinctively she headed for the cover of the trees and rocks. How long was twenty seconds? How long had she been running? She heard his voice, cheerfully loud, way up above her: 'Twenty! Coming ready or not.' And as he crashed his way down towards her, she saw a huge boulder shaped like a striking cobra, big enough to hide behind, big enough to give her time to catch her breath. Even as she paused, she noticed the tree beside the rock, with a fork in it just big enough to hold her foot. She might make it, might be able to swing herself onto the top of the rock. Some primeval instinct telling her that up was good. Slipping, 'Please, god, please,' slipping until her foot was suddenly secure and then up and scrambling, while she heard below, nearer and nearer, the devil himself whistling . . . then singing: *I'm a Yankee Doodle Dandy, Yankee Doodle do or die. A real life nephew of my Uncle Sam, born on the fourth of July.* Except he wasn't, of course. Just for a second she slipped out of fear, abstractly wondered why he wasn't singing 'Waltzing Matilda'. But he was whistling and singing while she flung herself on top of the rock, flat as she could, flat as a pancake, she hoped. Her hands feeling the rough porous warmth beneath her. Her fingers touching her cheek, warmed by the sun. Still alive. Not dead yet. She moved her hand down the outline of her body, as if to reassure herself. Felt a bump in her anorak pocket. Slipped her hand in – quietly, quietly – and felt her grip close around a knife. Of course! The knife. Carefully ran her finger along the blade. A question flitted across her mind, a dark shadow: Could she kill a man? Dismissed it. Don't ask. Don't answer. Best not to know. Clasped it in her hand.

★

'You're a clever little thing,' he called to her. Knew she could hear him. 'But I'll find you.'

Then silence, worse than the noise. She dared not raise her head. Hardly dared breathe. She could hear nothing, nothing at all. Could it be, could it possibly be that he couldn't find her? She moved her head a millimetre. Saw nothing, heard nothing. Dear god, how long can she lie here like this? Her left leg, in rebellion at the tension, twitched before she could stop it, and, oh Christ, she dislodged some dirt and a few loose flakes of rock. To her ears it sounded like an avalanche.

'Ha!' His voice exploded. 'Got you!' Up the tree and onto the rock even as she flung herself up. No advantage now. Facing each other. He crouched, grinning, and she realised as she waited that she hated him with every fibre of her being – there was nothing she wouldn't do to try and kill him, nothing she wouldn't try in order to stay alive. And as he lunged for her, she brought her knee up into his groin. But he was too quick, like lightning, grabbing her leg, forcing her down, so that all she could do – and did – was to scratch and claw and spit. 'A wild cat.' The grin never left his face. Never in doubt as to the outcome of this fight. 'I like that.' She kept fighting with her left hand, her right, slipping into the pocket, brought up the knife and into his shoulder. Easy. Like a knife into butter.

'Fuck!' It hit the air like gunshot, and as he grabbed his shoulder, she rolled from under him, crawling for the edge, heading for a jump into nothing, anything better than staying where she was. But he got her, grabbed her legs, brought her down again. She kicked and kicked, and felt – a miracle – no force on her feet, and simply rolled, rolled over the edge.

She landed on her back, stunned. Winded as if she'd fallen from a horse. She thought suddenly of the hundreds of times her pony ditched her and raced home without her. How much she used to hate it. How much now she wished it was a fall off her pony now. She blinked: *Where was he? . . . not far, she was sure . . .* She rolled again, under the ledge of the rock. She could hear him already. He wasn't coming straight after her. He was swearing and skittering down the shallow side, but he would be here soon enough. Did she have enough strength to run? Something told her, no, once she was in the open, he could shoot her easily enough, as easily, she thought wryly, as taking a photograph. She raised herself gingerly into a squatting position, then stood and backed towards the rock's spine. On top it had been warm and rough, underneath it was cool and damply dark. As she stood, her breath coming in short sharp gasps, a flicker of movement caught her eye, and thinking it was him, she whirled towards it.

The snake raised its head, stared at her, just a few inches away from her, so that now she was paralysed, and oh Jesus, if she thought she was scared before, it was nothing compared to this. It was the river all over again, the fear running through her body, as the creature watched her, unblinking.

He was down now. 'You fucking bitch.' He roared: 'I'll blow your fucking brains out.' Well, she knew *that*. Would almost rather that than snakebite. And the snake, distracted by the same noise, gliding out from the shade, gliding away from her, just as *he* came charging round the corner, so that he tripped on it, trod on it and it struck. But he was so cluttered up, so covered in khaki pockets and boots that it was hard to see if it had bitten him. Flailing on the ground, snake and human impossibly entwined, while he roared and bellowed.

As if it was nothing to do with her, as if this wasn't her chance to get away, she stood and watched, until he gasped, 'Help me, for fuck's sake, help me.' Her manners almost getting the better of her, she stretched her hand out towards him, while at the same time, the snake found a way out of the mess of limbs, and slid off, and at that split second she saw again the danger and from somewhere heard a voice, as clear as a bell: *He killed me and he killed my unborn child, and he will kill you too. What are you waiting for?*

(Does this sound extreme? Did I really hear Ellen's voice? What has always bothered me about this is that if I did hear it that time, why did she not speak to me before, or after, when things were so messy? I could have done with a kind word then. Over the years I have mostly persuaded myself that it was my imagination, or even simply my subconscious stressing the danger I was in . . . And yet, it was not my voice I heard, it was another woman's voice. The fact is I simply don't know, but I believe that the voice, from wherever it came, saved my life.)

So that now she leapt forward, the knife still in her hand, before he could rebalance, while he was still concentrating on whether he had been bitten. His back was towards her, exposed, vulnerable – he hadn't expected the fight to continue – at least not until he was ready to play cat and mouse again.

'What the . . .?'

She pushed the blade against his back. 'Don't move.'

'You wouldn't dare.'

'I did before.'

Silence and a slight tensing, and again Caroline heard the voice: *Yes, you did before and now you must again.*

'She was pregnant, you know,' Caroline told him.

'Who spun you that line?'

'Paul. He didn't know about you. She told him she was pregnant and they had a row. She wanted an abortion.'

He tried to turn, but she pressed the blade against him again. 'Don't move.'

'You're a fucking liar.'

'I might be. I might not. I think she came to break it off with you because she didn't know if it was yours or Paul's. I think she decided to have an abortion, and was going to stay and make it work with Paul. Or perhaps she was going to keep it and stay with Paul even if it was yours. Anyway, she didn't get a chance either way, thanks to you. And one thing I know is Paul had no idea about you two.'

Jim slumped forward suddenly. 'Jesus, oh Jesus.'

As he slumped, she noticed the blood oozing down around his armpit, blood she'd drawn. She raised her left hand as if to touch him, to comfort him.

'Were you bitten?'

He shook his head. 'I don't think so.'

'You were lucky.'

'Yes.'

(And then, this scene, the scene I have replayed for twenty years. The scene that is the heart of the matter.)

★

The way he suddenly turned so that the blade scraped use-lessly down his back, the way he went for her legs, to bring her down again. How, as her legs gave way and she fell back, the knife was pointing upwards and again she shoved, anywhere that she could, already a sense of déjà vu, the knife plunging again, but this time it was his chest, this time, he fell on her, and cried in pain, suddenly whimper-ing, oh god, she would do anything to stop him, pushed him off her, so that he rolled away from her, onto his back, his eyes glassy, blood soaking the front of his shirt. And the sound of him! She couldn't bear the sound of him. He reached up to her with one hand. 'Please,' he groaned. 'Please.'

And I backed away from . . . I shook my head, *no, no.* What did he want of me? To save his life? To shoot him? For some reason I have always thought he wanted me to shoot him. That is somehow what I understood at the time, but I couldn't. I couldn't bring myself to do it. I simply con-tinued to back away, while he lay there, his breath rasping and gurgling, until finally that noise also stopped, and I could tell, even from twenty yards away, I could somehow tell that he had died. And I didn't know then that I would have immense cause, only a few days later, to be extremely grateful that I did not shoot him. Although now even that seems like an irony because if I had shot him, I would have had to stand trial, and if I had waited for a trial, despite what would presumably have been the obvious outcome, I would have been in the country long enough for Paul to know I was pregnant.

(Actually, even for me to know I was pregnant. I still

did not suspect it. Would not suspect it for several months. I thought I had some strange stomach virus. I seemed to wake up feeling sick, but if I ate quickly enough it would pass. I missed two periods but even that didn't alert me; during times of stress or strain I had often missed one or two, and they had always been light anyway. Finally I went to see the doctor to complain about feeling so unwell and he enlightened me. I'd gone to see our family doctor in Woodstock. He thought it was amusing. 'I didn't think I'd have to explain the facts of life to someone of your age, Caroline,' he said, looking over his bifocals. If I'd known, I never would have gone to see him. I'd always favoured female doctors anyway; it was only because I thought it was a simple virus. But I'm skipping ahead.)

So what is the shadow that has hung over me for twenty years? Simply this: *Did Jim's actions bring about his own death? Am I, or was he, responsible for his death?*

The answer is, of course he was responsible, but I killed a man. I killed a man and it changed my life, and not for the better.

When his breathing had stopped, then finally I turned and ran, climbing up as fast as I could back towards the road, only stopping when I was sure, absolutely sure, that I was far enough away to be safe. Just in case. Just in case he was not dead. Which was also a recurring nightmare for many years. That he did not really die, and that he had come back to find me. It was much worse than *Carrie*.

I don't think I felt truly safe until Harry and I moved

into this flat and I was able to make it as secure as I wished. The first time my mother visited she was astonished.

'Why on earth have you got bars on the fourth floor?' she asked.

'All my photographic equipment, Mum,' I lied easily. 'It's just too valuable to lose it all.'

The perfect excuse which allowed me to lock, double lock and bar and security alarm the entire flat.

It allowed me my first terror-free nights for years, and I almost wept with relief. I had no idea that at the same time I was making my flat burglar proof I was attempting to ensure no-one would ever get past my own internal locks and bars.

'You were lucky.'

'Yes.'

'You were lucky.'

'Yes.'

'Please . . .'

His last words an affirmation and a request.

'Yes . . . please . . .'

But not so lucky. From her vantage point on the hill she could see his body. She clutched her arms around herself and rocked backwards and forwards, swaying in time to her sobs, and now, after all, she was the lucky one.

Chapter FOURTEEN

The camera makes everyone a tourist in other
people's reality, and eventually in one's own.

Susan Sontag

Wouldn't it be easy if that could be The End? After
all, you know my secret – that I killed a man – you
understand, I hope, the trauma I suffered. You know,
because I have told you, what happens next. You must, by
now, have come to the right conclusions – that I did not
stay in Australia, that Paul and I divorced and that I have
had no contact with him for nineteen years. By then Harry
was born, his birth registered: father unknown. Even my
solicitor did not know the truth. He thought we were
getting divorced because I had come back to England, had
an affair and got pregnant. I chose him carefully – a young,
unmarried male, unlikely to enquire too far into the messy
history of an older married woman, unlikely to care. As for
Paul, he had no idea and until last night with Luke I have

never felt he had any right to know. Why did I feel that? Because, quite simply, I have always thought he could have prevented the horror I went through. I felt let down by him, and I had come to understand that I could never, ever take Ellen's place. I did not want to be a substitute for a dead woman. I was angry – I think I still am – that he could dream of marrying me when his heart was still elsewhere. I simply cut the emotional connection. I have always been able to do that. If I don't like something, or somebody, I drop it. A person, once they have been wiped off my emotional map, holds no more interest for me than a brick – probably less, since I might find a brick interesting to photograph. And yet, this is not quite true is it? Because what I have harboured for years and years is anger.

Of course, there would have to be something about a brick, wouldn't there? Presupposing that an image contains meaning, and that meaning must be 'read' by the person receiving the image, I, as the photographer, would also first have to 'read' the brick; see something in it, traces of its former life perhaps, a line of moss, the fall of light and shade, a scratched initial, its placement somewhere unexpected. And I would hope as a photographer that my purpose in photographing the brick would be, if not obvious, then at least able to be understood by the viewer. Which is, in part, the problem with interpretation since we know, or come to know, that visible images are not necessarily understandable, especially if they come from a context outside the viewer's knowledge. Which is a way, I suppose, for me to wonder what on earth people at an exhibition in a south London gallery will make of images from 12 000 miles and twenty years away.

Blind Freddy of course could see where my ability to

detach comes from – I know that. It is both from and because of my father. When the first and most important male in your life leaves you without so much as a goodbye kiss, you have to make adjustments. Promised holidays in the exotic places he lived in that never eventuated, Christmas and birthday presents that arrived late, if at all. One year my mother even bought something for me and pretended it was from him because she could not bear to see my disappointment, but I knew that it was from her, although I never told her so.

Now I have to face the terrible fact that these are all excuses, half truths, blame apportioned in order for me to justify my action, the action which led to my estrangement from Harry, an estrangement which, whilst it appears to have mended, has left a vulnerable spot in both of us where before there was none.

When Harry woke me in the car, before my night with Luke, before I began to acknowledge that there was the slightest possibility I was wrong not to tell him about his father, we had, as I mentioned, a coffee together in the greasy spoon café near Karen's flat.

It was not an unmitigated success. How could it be? I couldn't bring myself to tell him the absolute truth. He asked me, several times, 'But what did he do to you that was so bad?' And I just shook my head. I couldn't answer. I couldn't say: 'It wasn't what he did to me, in the end, it was that I killed a man, and I felt I had to leave.' I gave him platitudes, I suppose, that I'd never intended to hurt him, that I wanted to protect him, that I'd made what I thought was the right decision for the right reasons. He stood up and pushed his chair away. 'But you've lied to me,' he said, and the tears started to his eyes. 'You've lied to me all my life, and I always thought you were someone who told the truth.'

'Harry.' I put out my hand towards him, but he just shook his head.

'I don't want to talk about it. I've got to go.'

And the rest, well you know the rest. I got to work late, in a fluster. I was angry with Harry by then. And then there was Luke and the row and the night, and as I lay there wide awake trying to find some pinpoint of light in the unravelling of my life, and at the same time marvelling in the presence of the man in my bed, I knew that I had to tell Harry the whole truth and nothing but the truth. He deserved to know. This time I persuaded him to come to the flat. It was awkward at first. He was like a visitor in his own home. I'd even tidied up for him! As if he would notice. But I told him. I told him everything. I showed him the photographs, I gave him this to read, and I talked to him about it all until finally there was nothing left to say. But I wasn't quite sure if we'd made it through, not until he yawned and stretched and said, 'God Mum, that's a hell of a story. I think I might turn in for the night.' And I realised that he meant here, with me, in his room. 'Sure, love,' I said. 'We can always talk more tomorrow.'

'Yes,' he said. 'Tomorrow.'

After he had gone to bed, as I was switching off lights and rinsing cups, it occurred to me that I have to do two more uncomfortable things before I am truly finished with this: I must make my peace with my father, and I must make my peace with Paul. Harry will want to know his father now, and I will have to swallow my stupid pride. I cannot go on being angry with them, not after all these years, and if it is my father from whom it stems then that is where the healing should take place. As for Jim, I do not forgive him – how could I? – but I will try very hard to persuade myself that not every man I meet is out to betray me in some way, or to abuse me, or worse – murder me. Perhaps it will work with Luke, perhaps with someone else. I know this, though: something has to shift.

But also, because of the nature of what I am writing, I am not quite finished yet, am I? I cannot quite walk away and leave Caroline sobbing there on the hill. I have a need to write it down. If it was a photograph it would be demanding to be printed, but these are words demanding to be written.

When Caroline got back to the road she walked around the truck several times. The passenger's door was still open. She slammed it shut but couldn't bring herself to climb in. It seemed obscene to touch the steering wheel. To touch anything where his hands had been. She rested against the spare tyre. Where on earth was she going to go? To the police, of course, to Bathurst. She would have to tell them what had happened. No question about that. No reason why she should change her plans long-term, however. No reason not to imagine at the time that she could get out of there.

What was I thinking? Autopsies, inquests, trials . . . none of these things occurred to me, not even for a second. I think I thought because I had killed a killer in self-defence, that they would bury him, and that would be that. I suppose the fact is I didn't stop to think at all.

But things had changed. Her husband was not a murderer. The murderer was dead. She would like to give Paul this information, would like him to know that Ellen had been revenged. She owed it to Paul to let him know that Jim was dead. And that Jim had killed Ellen. So once more she climbed into Jim's truck, once more she set off back towards Rock Forest, along the flinty track. As she drove, she put the final pieces of the jigsaw into place. Jim, despite the fact that he had murdered Ellen, or even because he had murdered Ellen, had planted the flowers because he loved her. As for Ellen, it seemed to Caroline obvious that she must have loved both the men in her life. Right to the end she had tried to protect both of them – Paul by not telling him about Jim; Jim by not telling him she was pregnant. The final piece of the jigsaw was this: What had Ellen been going to do? Caroline would never know. The jigsaw would always be missing this one piece. The only thing she could be certain of was that at least she had not married a murderer.

Wouldn't it be nice, too, if I could suddenly change the film . . . produce an alternate reality for us: happy snaps of Harry growing up, his proud parents smiling in the background. If I could tell you: 'Look, when I got back to the farm, we fell into each other's arms.'

In fact, I could tell you that and I wouldn't be lying.

★

As Caroline drove the last fifty yards down to the farmhouse, she realised that she was trembling all over, her hands were shaking so violently she could scarcely keep them on the steering wheel. It was all she could do to stop the truck under the old pine tree near the shearing shed.

The sound brought Paul out of the house.

The sound of the truck brought Paul out of the house, and he stood there by the door and waited while I walked down the hill towards him. I have often wondered why he waited. I suppose he must have been expecting Jim, and I suppose when he saw me he could hardly have guessed what I had just been through. But as I got closer to him he could see something was wrong, and by now I was crying, the tears unbidden, simply falling in the same way that my limbs were trembling, so that when he saw me, really saw me, then at last he came towards me and held out his arms, and I did literally fall into them. And although he still had no idea what had happened, he held me close and stroked my head, and said, 'Poor girl, poor Caroline . . . it's all right.'

And again I am forced to wonder while I remember this: is Luke right? Could we not have salvaged our marriage out of this? Paul loved me and stood by me and supported me in the next few weeks. I give him that absolutely. Why did I detach? Was it too painful to go on with him, with the person who knew the story? All these years I have persuaded myself that it was his fault I left, that he forfeited all rights with his behaviour, with his insistence that we even stay at the farm from the moment it went wrong. But I have a feeling that the truth is more mundane than the story. I think that at some point over the next few weeks while he was being solicitous and kind and helping me through the quagmire we suddenly both found ourselves in – after all it meant proving that Jim had killed Ellen as well – I decided it was all too hard and that I must, at all costs, get home. And once I was back in England, then came my pregnancy, and I became certain that I was right, that I should stay and that he would not know he had ever fathered a child.

Chapter FIFTEEN

Choice of developer has to be related to film characteristics. For example, it is futile to shoot on a fast, coarse-grain emulsion and then hope that by processing in fine-grain developer the result will be equivalent to a fine-grain film. The best results occur from matching the developer to the film. Mismatches are generally counterproductive, but there are times when a film is known to be under- or overexposed, and choice of a particular developer can correct results.

Paraphrased from The Photographer's Handbook,
by John Hedgecoe

I tell my students: there is as much art in printing as there is in taking the original photograph. I love the process of printing. I love the names of all my objects – the developing tank, the processing tank, the reel loader, the mono baths and sheet film and dowels and antistatic backing. Burners, timers, dodgers, fixer, frame, enlarger. It took me years to create the perfect darkroom. I can't begin to describe the excitement of waiting for an image to emerge – all of which is likely to be lost, of course, now that digital cameras are improving all the time, and negatives can be stored straight into computers. It's like the difference between home-cooked food and takeaway food, even the gourmet takeaway food available today. It is the *process* of cooking that is pleasurable and grounding, the mixing of ingredients, the satisfaction of watching the final dish emerge. Likewise with printing. How sad not to have that pleasure.

Harry does not agree with me on this. He tells me I'm oldfashioned. I said to him, Do you realise some newspapers these days don't even store negatives, only the ones that get in the paper? Think, I said, of all those wonderful potential images, think of the gold that's being thrown out, the waste of it all. He shrugged. Well they can't all keep them, Mum, he said, the world would drown in images.

There would be worse ways to go, I said.

Luke was impressed when I showed him my darkroom. 'God,' he said. 'You could live in here.' And then he laughed. 'So this is where you run and hide.'

I was about to get offended, but he pulled me to him. 'Shhh,' he said. 'Don't get angry. I'm just jealous. You should see my darkroom. It's a tip, it's such a mess.'

I have plunged into the printing process at last, and, at last, I have an idea for the major work. Which leaves me only a matter of days to complete it.

Harry has moved back home. Or, at least, he has moved

back home and moved back out again, but this time it was a harmonious leaving.

I have visited my father, and my mother's grave, and my father is coming to the exhibition opening.

Paul is coming to the exhibition opening.

Luke has read this manuscript and taken offence at my description of fashion photography. Luke is coming to the exhibition opening.

Harry, for whom this was written, has read it, or most of it. Harry is coming to the exhibition opening.

Paul – did I mention it before? – is coming to the exhibition opening.

I will have an ex-husband, a father, a son and a current lover at my exhibition opening. I will not have a mother, I do not have a sister, but I will have loved ones and family and my close friends.

And now I feel as if I have my own jigsaw puzzle in front of me, or to be more precise, two jigsaw puzzles. One is the work, but that in a sense is a puzzle I understand – that this negative hasn't come up as I imagined it might, but this other one has produced a small treasure, and in which order should they be hung, these photographs that tell without telling my secret? But this is teasing work, almost pleasurable. The other jigsaw puzzle is surely the hardest. The map of my heart and where it has been on its journey through life, where it has come from, where it is now, where it is going. Who am I now, now that the secret is told?

I think I thought that if I saw my father, it would help. I'm not sure why. After all, it never has before. But at least, this time, we approached something like communication, and perhaps I took the biggest step of all – I stopped expecting him to give me what I want.

It was six months since I had seen him and he had aged twenty years. I could hear him coughing as I walked up the path to the little townhouse he shares with Trudy, his wife. (This too has been a source of contention to me over the years. When they finally returned from living their strange expatriate life in Spain and the south of France, they bought a place twelve miles away from where my mother lived. I said to him at the time: 'You've got the whole of England to live in and you want to live on our patch.' He was offended. 'I thought you'd like it if I was nearby.'

'Why?' I asked. 'Why on earth would I like it?' Which produced the inevitable explosion and the inevitable fight.

But of course, he has tried to be a good grandfather, I'll give him that. In fact he has been a much better grandfather than he was father. And over the years I learnt to keep quiet when Harry would sing his praises. But here's a thing – I was jealous, jealous of my own child. That my father could remember his birthday, give him lavish presents, spoil him at Christmas. I began to curtail the visits – I fudged it with Harry when he asked – too busy, someone not well, clashing engagements. He was always so sad not to see his grandfather that sometimes, just for a minute, guilt would set in but I could reason it away soon enough, and it wasn't as if he never saw him. It served me no purpose in the end because as soon as Harry was old enough he would hop on a train to visit with them anyway, and how could I express my displeasure and my envy without sounding hysterical? So I kept it quiet. It wasn't until Harry was at college that he even thought to question my relationship with my father.

I wonder – could anybody reading this be able to tell that these last few paragraphs have now been sitting there for several weeks? I have discovered I would rather do almost anything than write about my father. Even my Australian experience pales into insignificance. Why? Why should it be so hard? In the last few weeks I have thrown myself into an orgy of housecleaning, of furniture moving. In fairness this last perhaps to protect myself from the pain of Harry's leaving.

Not that his leaving was unpleasant, it was just, as he explained to me, that he and Karen had discovered they enjoyed being in her shared place so much they thought they might move into a small place together. 'We might pool resources,' he said wisely.

The 'resources', I quickly discovered, included me. If I would increase his allowance, he thought he might be able to get by. He could get a part-time job in the local bookshop near college, not much money, but a huge discount on all the books he needed and flexible hours . . . and so it went on. What could I say? He'd obviously made his mind up and if I was to honour in any way the friendship we had always had, then it did not behove me to make a fuss.

'You'll be all right, Ma,' he said cheerfully as soon as he could see there wouldn't any opposition. 'Anyway, you've got Luke now.'

I wanted to cry out, Harry, that's not the point, I don't know who or what he is to me yet, but you are my only child, my one true love, the sole force that kept me connected to this planet in the dark days when I came home to England full of fear and nightmares. I wanted to tell him, It was because of you I kept on living, because of you I made myself become sane again.

Because there was a time there for a while when not

only was I not quite sane, but, looking back from a distance, I think perhaps I was almost mad.

Which perhaps raises the question to which anyone, I suspect, reading this would want to know the answer. If you have killed someone, how do you avoid being charged with murder?

The simple answer is that you don't.

We went – we had to – to Bathurst police station, to report what had happened. It was while we were sitting there, waiting to see the detective on duty, that something happened to me. The only way I can describe it is that I somehow left my body. It was as if my nervous system, after my fight to my near death, was in overload. I had become incapable of taking on anything more, and as vivid as every single memory is right up until that point, the time between then and when I finally made it to England is like an impressionistic blur, a splash of vivid colour here and there, a snatched memory of words, words, words. My words to the police, theirs to me. Of course, I had to be arrested. I had killed a man. It was my word against a dead man. And he wasn't talking.

Except. Except he was in a sense.

These things saved me: the autopsy revealed that Jim had enough snake venom in him to kill him; and thanks to the slowness of life in the country, the old Landrover was still sitting at the back of the police court car park a year later. Although it had been checked, it was easy for them, now they knew what they were looking for, to find it, and they did.

And then: the luckiest thing of all. The recently appointed detective was – how shall I put it? – not a fan of Jim's. Not at all. It came out, not all at once, not by any means, but gradually, over the next few days, that he had his suspicions. He thought Jim had stretched his job description way beyond the boundaries. He wanted to know how the parks personnel had managed to overlook the fact that after his discharge from the army, Jim had been one of the most problematic of the prospectors who ended up at Rock Forest, always in fights; then some trouble over a girl who said he had raped her, although she had never laid charges; and then the latest complaint, the one Jim thought I had laid, from someone who said he had been disturbed in the night by his dogs and had gone out to see what the racket was, just in time to catch a glimpse of a thickset man leaping into a van – and there he was twenty sheep down. He was sure it was Jim. Jim had been the only one who knew he should have been in Sydney that day for his daughter's birthday but then she'd rung to say one of the kids was sick and why didn't he come the next week. What's more, he told the detective, two of his gates were missing.

I remember that at that I laughed. I think he told us all this when I was out on bail, when it had begun to become apparent that I would not have to stand trial, that there were all sorts of ways they could fudge it, and would. Not that they told me this, but, my lawyer said, that was what he was coming to understand. There were all sorts of reasons why it would be embarrassing if there was a trial: for the police because they had always simply assumed Ellen died in an accident; for the parks department who had given Jim the job; for the government, because the parks department came under the state government; and because it would have meant publicity for Ellen too, and

Paul did not want that. It was enough, he said, let it rest. Let her rest.

But when they told me about the gates, I couldn't help laughing. I remember everybody in the room looked at me. 'But don't you see,' I told them. 'The very idea that someone who works for the parks and wildlife department is mad enough to steal gates. It's funny.' They seemed embarrassed for me, as if by laughing I had done something shameful, but then they weren't to know that I had left my body some days before.

What I held onto throughout it all was this: that I would one day soon get on a plane and fly away from it all, from the whole situation and from Paul as well. In the meantime I went around pretending I was there. I was polite and friendly and cooperative, and even in a vague sort of way loving towards Paul, although we didn't make love. No, he seemed to sense that I was not ready for that. I'm sure he thought that once life was back to normal we'd be all right. He'd talk about plans. He wanted to sell the farm, not unnaturally. We'd buy a big house in Sydney, maybe take a few months off and travel, and I would agree and discuss it animatedly, and all the time wonder how long it would be before I could escape, and how long the strange sickness in my stomach would go on.

It was as if I was swimming in some viscous liquid that only I was aware of. As if there was a filter between me and other people so that whatever they did, or said, did not really touch me; and all the time there was this sensation of my physical body being left below me to do all these things, while the rest of me hovered in the greyness above, detached and unreachable – even by me. I honestly don't think I came back into my body until after the doctor had told me I was pregnant. I remember that I drove back to my mother's place, and crawled into bed, and began to cry.

So what do these memories serve at the moment? Still a way to avoid writing about him, perhaps. Or a way of at least attempting to figure my way through to a resolution. Perhaps where he is concerned, I should just plunge in.

'You look well,' the father said.

'So do you,' she lied.

He shrugged. 'I'll do, I s'pose. Come in.'

Already she wanted it to be different. She wished that he had moved to cuddle her, or that she had gone to him and kissed him. Already it was too late.

They walked into the house together. Her father's wife rushed towards her and enveloped her in the hug that should have occurred between them. 'How lovely to see you, dear . . .'

She made reciprocal noises. Nice new curtains . . . the roses are lovely this year . . . how's life in the village?

And that's how it went. All through lunch. Every now and then my father would go into a paroxysm of coughing, and my stepmother would put the oxygen mask on for him. We took no notice of the fact that he hardly ate, that after only a few minutes he went back to his armchair. We talked about the weather, the garden, the Irish Question, the Middle East Question, the Balkans Question. We touched on the subject of Harry and left the subject of Harry's father well alone. We made no reference to our non-speaks, or to my fury at his interference, or at Harry's disappearance. We ate roast lamb, or at least Trudy and I did, and apple pie and had cups of tea in their sitting room with its dainty antimacassars and strange curios from their travels: Spanish dancing dolls and bowls from Provence, mixed with Cotswold cottages and pot pourri. It was always one of the things I held against Trudy, her lack of taste. I could never understand how my father could leave a person with consummate taste and end up with someone so, I don't know, *twee*. At the same time I can still hear my mother's voice berating me for some judgement I had passed on one of the girls at school. 'I might not want you to say serviette, but there is no need to look down on people who do.'

In the end, with the afternoon shadows lengthening, I thought that perhaps I could at last make my getaway, and I said, Well, that was lovely, and now I must be going, it's a long drive back. It was Trudy, not my father, who said, Must you? You could always stay the night. If it had been him, might I have stayed? Perhaps, although probably not. I suspect I would have found the pleasure of rejecting him too great. Not something I am proud to admit.

Until, at the very last when we were standing by the car – all jolly smiles, and wasn't that lovely – Trudy said: 'Oh, I forgot dear, I made Harry some peach chutney and you some damson jam', and she dashed inside, so that Dad and I were left together, fidgeting together. *And inside my heart was breaking. Give me a sign, I thought, give me a sign that you actually care.* I looked at his face, so old and lined, and his eyes were so sad that finally I realised, he is waiting for a sign *from* me. And I coughed and cleared my throat and said, So ... Dad ... will you come to the exhibition? If you're well enough? And I waited for some sort of putdown, for the inevitable sarcastic remark, but he looked me straight in the eye and said, I'd love to come ... if I'm still around. Oh Dad, I said, don't say that, and I stepped forward towards him. He was still for a moment, his arms limp at his sides, and then almost like a toy soldier he lifted them, and opened them to me.

In the end I fear that this will have to be enough for both of us. Standing there, our arms awkwardly around each other, me crying unseen tears into the shoulder of his jacket, quickly wiping my eyes as Trudy came dashing back again, wreathed in smiles. How nice to see the pair of you like that ... let me take a picture. Both of us stepping back in horror. No Trudy, said Dad, for Christ's sake. And for once I was in complete agreement with him. I gave him a big grin. I'll see you both then, at the opening, I said, and he grinned back. It isn't a lot to live on, it isn't much to replace forty-odd years of misunderstandings, but it'll have to do. That's what I thought as I drove back towards Woodstock.

I don't put flowers on my mother's grave. I don't like the idea that they will sit there and wilt and die. What I do is I take a few stones with me, stones I pick up from every place I visit. Sometimes I may even remove some and plant them somewhere that takes my fancy, or take them back home to rejoin my collection. It's become a ritual. I do it for a reason, of course. Mum loved stones. I think as a speleologist she was also a natural geologist. She was fascinated by the earth. I had more lectures on palaeobotany, the Palaeocene era and palaeoecology than I care to remember – and those are only three of the words I had to recite over and over. She never said she was disappointed in my lack of interest in caves but I guess she must have been. I always thought it was a bizarre thing to do – out in all weathers in cold, damp, dark places. But she would often bring back stones or flints or fossils, and I would draw or photograph them for her. Her archivist, she called me, before Dad's departure made her more or less home-bound.

But I did share her love of stones. I've collected stones from everywhere. I have little cairns all around the flat. I put them around pot plants, on mantelpieces and shelves and bookshelves. Every stone holds a memory for me: this beautiful day on the beach with Harry, this assignment in Cyprus, this picnic lunch at Richmond. Sometimes a stone will call me and I'll pick it up and cradle it for a while, maybe photograph it.

I remember the river stones at Rock Forest, stones of every shape and size and grade, of black and white and grey and brown and speckled and striped and spotted. As I was leaving the flat for the last time, on my way to the airport, I stopped at the doorway and turned around, and saw them there, the little beauties I had brought up from the river that day: Paul had told me that as well as the gold that would wash down the river, there were hundreds of precious and semiprecious stones. But it was a high strike out rate, he said, in answer to my question as to why there weren't hordes of people looking for a way to make money, that's why the river banks weren't full of people vandalising stones for possible riches. Also, he said, not a lot of people realised Australia's creek beds had this untold wealth sitting there. A friend of his on a nearby property had found a ruby.

Caroline looked around the flat one last time. Despite her time there, there was nothing that spoke of her presence, or even Paul's. It had remained neutral. A place planned by someone else for a different life that didn't eventuate, and now she too was leaving it. She spotted the stones on the window sill, the ones she tinkered with whenever she sat in the window looking out over the bay and the boats below, wondering and wondering about what had happened to her and where exactly it was that she had gone, and why exactly she couldn't come back from it, wherever *it* was. She walked over and picked them up one by one, measuring their smooth weight, their coolness, and slipped a couple into her jacket pocket. Why she couldn't quite say, a talisman perhaps, the smallest of reminders. After all, it was not as if she was taking anything else with her.

Not as if I was taking anything else. But of course I had Harry, growing and growing inside. Growing up a storm, as it happened. Almost a ten-pound baby. We hardly fitted, him and me, although we managed in the end, with the help of teams of people. Not exactly your natural birth. Mum seemed to think I was on a caving expedition. Go in there and breathe, she admonished me from time to time, don't be afraid of the dark. At one stage I remember screaming at her, I'm not a fucking speleologist, I'm giving birth to a fucking elephant. The nurses looked most surprised as I recall, but Mum took it in her stride. There

there, dear, she said, it'll be over soon. Which it wasn't.

And the other thing I brought back – those visual memories, my films. I didn't even develop the films in Australia,
I didn't even think about it. I had, as they say, other things
on my mind. In fact for the first time in my whole career
those rolls of film sat and collected dust for years. Every
now and then I would tell people I had been out in
Australia for a year, never saying exactly when (I didn't
want Harry to add two and two) and every now and then
I would print a roll, but I couldn't look at them, not really,
not up until now. I had no way of seeing them beyond
the story I have told. It came in front of every image and
destroyed them.

Even now that I have begun to *see* them, I do not think
they are my best work, but there is something about them;
a sense of isolation, of emptiness and, I hope, almost of the
slightest hint of danger, that is interesting. That is it: I think
they are interesting, finally. Which could be worse.

Who knows what the critics will say, however. They
have their own ways of seeing. Sometimes they startle me
with their insight, sometimes they startle me with their lack
of it. Luke thinks they will like them. Makes a change from
all that urban stuff, he said. It'll appeal to the bushranger
in them.

Luke. Now that is another question.

So that is where I went. To my mother's grave with stones
from Australia in my pocket, and a grin from my father in
my heart.

I had a special stone, one of Harry's, for her as well. I
told him, I'm going to see Mum, do you want me to take

a stone? Sure, he said, why not. Give her my love.

Give her my love. Just like that. I think I must have done something right to have a son who does not mind sending his love to a dead person.

So I did send his love. I tidied the stones, and resorted the piles, and when they were done I sat and carefully placed my Australian offering and Harry's stone with them. I weeded the nettles and dandelions that were encroaching, and all the time I talked to her about everything that had happened to me in the last few months. It would be nice to say I felt heard, or understood, or even comforted, but it would be going too far; and although she was always supportive when I needed it, it was not as if she was that kind of mother when she was alive. There there, was about the closest she got to real sympathy. You couldn't expect someone who liked to camp out and whose idea of fun was to spend several days underground with minimal food and comfort to be well versed in the art of reflective listening, or even perhaps in simple understanding. But I did feel somehow relieved. Almost as if I hadn't spoken to her on the phone for a long time and needed to catch up with her. I told her I wished she could come to the exhibition, but then I laughed. Perhaps on second thoughts that's not a good idea, I said, after all Dad might just make it there himself. I wondered what would happen after he died. Would he join her in death where he hadn't in life? They were married a long time, after all. Much longer than I've ever managed.

Which brings us back to Luke again. Because, here's the thing, I said to him the other day, Look, I don't know if I can do this. I've gone this long and the longest live-in relationship I've ever had was less than a year, and none of the others, even the ones that lasted some considerable time, ever really lived with me. I actually don't know if I can do this.

Well, that's all right, he said. Because I know how to. I'll show you. But, I said, you got divorced. Yes, he said. After twenty-five years, and it was amicable on both sides.

Which is surprising but seems to be true. He doesn't have a problem talking to his ex-wife, or his daughters for that matter. We met the daughters, Alison and Louise, for a coffee in Battersea Park. It is strange to see your lover suddenly a father – even though, of course, his children are quite grown-up, twenty-three and twenty-one. They teased him and he took it in good part, although he suddenly looked more rumpled, a bit more careworn, as if even the very idea of children was enough to age you, however old they were. But there was genuine love there, you could see that. It startled me so to witness it. I suppose my father and I have wasted all these years getting at each other – and then of course let's not mention Harry with no father – so I have had very little experience of fatherhood in that regard.

They seemed to like me, although it was hard to tell. But they chatted and were friendly, and gave us both hugs when they left. We'll have you to dinner soon, I said, you can come and meet my son and his girlfriend, and they didn't seem fazed by it. Cool, they said, when we dropped them at the Tube. At the last moment, Louise turned and waved, Oh, she said, I forgot, Mum says hi. Tell her I say hi right back, Luke shouted. And she nodded and smiled.

It bothered me. I thought this must be the hidden agenda revealing itself. I was almost ready to be angry again. Luke said, There's no point looking like a thundercloud.

She's allowed to mention her mother. She's probably feeling a bit insecure. It's nothing to do with you. It wouldn't have mattered who it was.

I wish sometimes he wouldn't be so goddamn right, and so I told him.

Over breakfast one morning we started talking about the things we could do together. My imagination stretched to a few days in Cornwall, but Luke was off and running. We could sell my flat, he said, and yours and buy a house somewhere with plenty of room for two darkrooms. Or we could sell mine and go and travel for a year, or leave our jobs, or ... I don't know ... anything – the world is our oyster.

I could feel this terror building up inside me. I couldn't speak with it. It sat like a ball in the middle of my throat. He turned to me. What's wrong?

You're terrifying me, I said. Don't terrify me. I'll have to run away. Even if I don't want to.

He came and sat beside me and put his hand on my knee. That's okay, he said, we'll live like we are for the rest of our lives, you in your flat, me in mine. We'll stay at the college until we're old and grey, or older and greyer, and we'll undertake absolutely never to suggest that we might live together.

You're teasing me. I felt like a caged bird now, all fluttery and caught.

I'm not. He smiled. It's up to you, you know, it's up to us. We can do it however we like, it doesn't matter. We can combine your naturally suspicious nature with my overly gullible one and we'll be a perfect pair.

That's the point, he said, of being a pair. You talk about things and you come to a decision that suits you both.

Find a way to make it not scary, I said.

He thought about it. Look, you do it with Harry, don't you? You've always been there for him. You've always been committed to him. It's simple, once you're committed, the rest is simple. You just say you want to be with me, I just say I want to be with you – the rest is just living, that's all, muddling through, getting by, getting on, having quarrels, making up. It's simple.

Simple?

Simple. Look, he said, again, and this time he was quiet about it. I want to be with you, but in the end if you don't want to be with me, I'll get over it, and I'll find someone else. I like sharing my life with someone. I was happy to be married to Kaye, we had great times over the years. I've been happy to be by myself, but now I'm ready to share again, and I'd like it to be with you. He laughed. Christ knows why! Caroline, it's simple. After all, how many nights a week are we actually spending apart at the moment? It's just the idea that we're not living together that's keeping you from having to acknowledge that that's what we're doing.

Ouch. That hurt. And the other stuff. That hurt too. My suspicious nature et cetera. Look at the bars on this place, he said. It's like Alcatraz. No-one can break in, but no-one can get out either.

Don't for a second think I'm making him Mr Perfect though. That gullibility he told me about – he'll trust anybody. He puts things down in crowded places and then is surprised when people steal them; he lends money to people and then is surprised when they don't pay it back. He's messy and doesn't fold his clothes. What's going to happen, he said to me one night, if I don't fold them? They'll get … rumpled, I said. He laughed out loud. Oh no, rumpled clothes, he said. What a disaster.

It's all very well for you, I grumbled. My friend Jill says it's the Virgo in my chart. I have to have neatness around me, or it drives me crazy.

Well that's the end of us then, he said, hopping into bed. How sad. Astrologically incompatible. He stroked my nipples. What a shame, when we fit together so perfectly in every other way.

Can I live with a messy person? Can I live without bars? Can I simply say I want to be with someone? Is it really that simple? Sometimes I wonder about Kaye. He's told me a bit.

They split up because Luke got bored with fashion (thank goodness). She was a model, he was a fashion photographer when they met. She was clever as well as beautiful, he said. A nice combination. She opened a small homeware shop, very stylish, and it took off. They were happy, successful, had two healthy children, two great jobs. But, said Luke, she always wanted more. In the end it was too much for me, he said, the difference between us. One shop turned into two which turned a small chain – she sold out, made a fortune and started again. I thought we'd have more time together, but it's not what she wants. She's been a good mum, I'll give her that, but one day I realised she wanted to be successful more than she wanted the marriage to work. And me, I was disappointing her. I felt I'd done all the fashion work I ever wanted to. I wanted something – I'd got to the stage where I felt I wanted to put something back into the universe. She couldn't understand that at all. So we decided on a trial separation. And there we are. We both got out of it and realised it was over. Friendly but over.

It's sad, I told him. That it should just disintegrate like that.

I was sad, he said. So was she. But we knew we were right.

Chapter SIXTEEN

The virtue of the camera is not the power it has
to transform the photographer into an artist, but
the impulse it gives him to keep on looking.
Brooks Atkinson, Once Around the Sun

Paul rang, of course, when I got back from Australia.
He couldn't understand why I'd gone.

Won't you at least come back and we can try again, he
asked me. Please?

He was distraught at first. He rang every day, until I
wouldn't speak to him at all. Finally my mother thrust
the phone at me. He's not my husband, he's yours, she
said. In the end I had to be crueller than I wanted to
be, just to get rid of him. I told him, I don't want to
have anything to do with you, ever again, can't you
understand that?

Well, he said, I may as well be dead.

He chose the wrong person to say that to. Too many

179

dramatic walkouts from my father for that one to have any effect.

If that's how you feel, I said.

It is, he said. He put the phone down and that was the last time we spoke, at least until the other day.

It wasn't hard to find his number. He was obviously still in the small law firm he and his partner had all those years ago — it was a different address, somewhere in the city, but it was his name.

Harry wanted to be there when I called him.

I don't think that's such a good idea, I said. I thought, What if his father doesn't want to know, or won't speak to me, how will he feel then?

I said, I have to do this on my own, Harry. This is my stuff.

But he's my *father*, he said.

Yes, but he doesn't know that. You've had time to get used to the idea, he hasn't. You'll have to let me handle it first.

I'm not sure that 'handle it' is quite the right expression, but I did my best.

I had a list written down in front of me as a way in, if you like, in case I lost my nerve. Which I almost did. I remembered his voice as soon as I heard it, a firm clear voice, a good voice for a lawyer's, I always used to think. He sounded just like he did when I knew him. It flashed an image of him into my mind, his tall angular frame, the cowlick that he had passed on to his son. I could see him laughing at me in the early days, before we went to the farm. We were in the park below his flat. I can't remember what I'd said, but he was laughing and the sun was shining behind him, and even at the time I had thought that I would always like to remember him like this. And here it was and I had not thought of that memory for over twenty years, and now it was in my mind and as fresh and crisp as the day it happened. And all that ran through my mind without me being even able to say hello, so that in the end, the voice became exasperated.

'Is there anybody there?' he said.

'Hi.' I wondered if he might recognise my voice, make my job easier. But he simply said: 'Can I help you?'

'Paul?'

'Yes?' His voice was curious now, rather than cross.

'It's me. Caroline.'

Now here's the rub. He paused. 'Caroline who?' he said. Did he mean it? Had he really forgotten me? Later he said, Look, I have so many clients, you could have been anybody. I had to remind myself, as I had said to Harry, that he was not sitting thinking of me in Sydney in the same way I had been thinking of him. He was not poring over old photographs, exorcising his demons on paper, obsessively going over whether to speak to him or not.

He was simply, as it happened, living his normal life.

When finally he grasped it, it was hard to tell, but he seemed pleased. 'Caroline. My god, how are you?'

And so we talked a while. He told me he was married again, two children, teenagers now, two girls. How extraordinary, I thought. Two lives had been created over there and I had never heard of them to this day, and then there was this one, this other one that he had no idea about. He asked about me. I told him about the college, about the exhibition, about Luke. *I couldn't bring myself to talk to him about Harry.*

But then I said to him, 'Would you have liked a boy?' He said, 'Yes, I would ... we both would have ... but that's okay. They come along and you wouldn't change them for the world.' And then he said, 'And how about you? Have you had children?' The best I could think of to say was: 'In a sense.'

'What do you mean? Did you adopt?'

'Not exactly.' I could feel my heart pounding, that old sense of my body pulling away.

'I'm curious,' he said.

So I told him. I told him, 'When I came back to England, Paul, I was pregnant. And that child is now a young man called Harry. He's twenty-one, and he looks just like you.'

And there was a silence that went on so long I didn't know whether he had hung up or what. I said, 'Are you there?'

His voice was different. Harsh, almost cold. 'It could have been Jim's, couldn't it? How do you know it was mine?'

'I never slept with Jim.'

'How do I know that?'

'How do I know you never slept with him?'

Caroline could hardly believe it. Is this what he had thought all those years, that she too, like Ellen, had succumbed to Jim? It was like a blow in her stomach.

'Isn't that really why you left, because you discovered your

182

lover was a killer, and you were forced to kill him. It was really nothing to do with me, was it? Was it, Caroline?'

'It was everything to do with you.'

I so wanted to slam that phone down. I so wanted to walk away from it, that if it hadn't been for the fact that it was for Harry, I would have. It was the first time in my life I have truly had to swallow my pride. Perhaps one day it will prove to be a useful experience, although it's hard to imagine how. But I held on, I held on for grim death while I talked him through all of it. I did not put the phone down. I did not walk away. I did not even shout. What did I expect? I thought after. He was left in the dark, to come to his own conclusions, and perhaps if I had had any idea that they were so wrong, maybe I would have stayed in touch. I could hear his pain, as raw as the day he last spoke to me, as if nothing had happened in the meantime, and I acknowledged it at last – I have some culpability here, I had a responsibility and I avoided it. And as I thought that, it was as if a huge boulder was lifted from my chest, as if the act of asking for forgiveness was enough for me to truly receive it.

'I'm so sorry,' I said. 'So very, very sorry.'

He was not necessarily gracious in his acceptance of my apology, but it was a start. And in the end he said, 'So this son of mine . . . Harry? Is he there? Can I talk to him?'

And I knew we'd won through. I said to him: 'He's really yours, you know. You can take a paternity test if you like, but as soon as you see him, you'll know he's yours. There's no doubt about it.'

★

183

No doubt about it. Except that I had pretended all those years that he had nothing to do with his father, and now it all seemed so absurd, as if I had been living behind a curtain of chainmail, the first chink of which had been pierced when Harry had run away from me.

When Harry came back, after we'd talked in the café, when we attempted to pick up our lives until it became obvious that it wasn't going to work, it was as if a dam had broken. He was full of questions. What was his father like? Where did he live? When had I last spoken to him?

At one point he said, almost admiringly, That was a hell of a secret to keep for twenty years, Mum.

True.

And so they spoke, the father and the son, and Paul was moved enough to want to come and meet him straight away. 'You could come for Mum's exhibition,' Harry said, while I shook my head – no, no, no – but they had it all decided in a matter of minutes and that was that.

The night Harry officially left, the night he moved all his things out of the flat and into Karen's place, I said to Luke, I can't stay here, can we go to your place?

His flat, or warehouse, I should say, was as unbarred as mine was barred, as messy as mine was tidy – as male as mine was female, I suppose. I looked in the fridge, there was a piece of cheese rind, a lonely chili, and half a bottle of wine. Now, that's an interesting meal, I laughed. No stomach aches in that lot.

He was unashamed. That is one of the things I like –

no, love – about him, is that he is unashamed, whereas I have spent most of my life in a state of shame, for one reason or another. That night, just before I fell asleep I thought, How odd, my grown child is spending his first night officially away from home with his girlfriend, and his mother is spending her first night away from her flat in years with a man. Somehow what could have been one of the worst days of my life had turned into one of the best, and for once I felt no shame. In fact, I felt a curious sensation in my body which I tried to identify as I lay there, drifting off, and I was most astonished when it made its presence felt as the gossamer touch of optimism.